The Clairvoyant's Glasses

Volume 2

By Helen Goltz

Atlas Productions

Atlas Productions
Greenslopes QLD 4102
Web: www.atlasproductions.com.au

 A catalogue record for this book is available from the National Library of Australia

Proofread by Penny Clarkson

Beta-reader: Mary Fuxa

Cover design by Karri Klawiter – Art by Karri.

For Mary Fuxa

You fought the good fight and won, bravo!

Volume 2

Time has a shadow.

Chapter 1

Sophie Carell looked down at the dress she was wearing; she had selected it for an audition, which she now would not make. It was too cheery for a crime scene. Beside her, Detective Murdoch Ashcroft lightly tapped his fingers on the steering wheel. She stole a glance at him as he stopped tapping, pushed his hand through his dark hair, and returned it to the steering wheel. She knew he was a man who didn't like to be read, but his anxiety came off him in waves as they drove to the crime scene.

'Everything okay?' she asked.

'Sure. Thanks for this,' he said. 'I know you really wanted to audition for that part, sorry about the timing.'

Sophie gave a small shrug. 'Parts come and go, missing kids, not so. The parents must be terrified.'

He nodded.

'Although, I reckon I was a shoo-in for the role.' She smiled and brushed a strand of her wavy blonde hair behind her ear.

'Goes without saying,' he grinned. 'So, it's been a month

now. You were going to decide whether to stick with the fortune-telling or throw it in. Come to any conclusions?' He put the car's indicator on to pull off the freeway and, taking the turn, headed to the home of the parents of the missing five-year-old girl, the Kingsleys.

'To stay or not to stay,' Sophie said melodramatically, bringing her stage skills to the fore. 'Fortune-telling, huh?'

'Okay, it's a little more than that,' he conceded.

'Are you missing Aunt Daphne? Do you want me to continue or return to acting?' She teased.

'I do miss the old girl,' Murdoch admitted. 'But even I can't bring her back from the dead. There's room in my heart for both of you.' He gave her a wink.

Sophie laughed. 'Good of you.' She didn't answer his question and Murdoch gave her no encouragement to choose either career. The gift of special glasses bequeathed to her by her eccentric great aunt, Daphne Shelby, had changed her life. They had given her clairvoyance skills, and all the baggage that came with it. It had made for a daunting month, especially when she had been convinced her future was acting on the stage, not reading futures.

'Are you enjoying it?' he asked, prompting Sophie again.

'Surprisingly, yes. When Aunt Daphne told me I was going to follow in her footsteps as a clairvoyant, I have to tell you, it cheesed me off. But what I've achieved with the *gift* in the past month has given me more satisfaction than I've felt for a long time,' she said in a quiet voice.

'It's been good for me too, thanks,' he said, remembering the recent case she helped him solve. 'My partner's not as keen on using outside resources,' he said diplomatically, 'but Gerard never was a fan of Daphne's either, so it's not personal.'

She grimaced. 'I can't say I care too much about what Detective Gerard Oakley thinks. I've seen his future.'

'Yeah?' Murdoch's interest was piqued. 'What's going to happen to the old bastard?' he asked with a chuckle.

'Nothing terrible. But he won't be around for much longer... his retirement is pending and after a handshake and send off, he's going to go caravanning with his wife.'

'He'll like that, that's good.' Murdoch sobered.

'Where is he, by the way?' Sophie asked.

'Interviewing people at the shopping centre where the girl went missing. We're almost there.'

'What more can you tell me about the little girl?' Sophie asked.

'Not a great deal. I only just got called to the job. But when it comes to abductions, history tells us that the first few hours are crucial.'

'I understand, so where is the family now?'

'Her parents and another two older siblings were initially taken to the police station, but they've been taken home in case there is a call. A ransom... they're not short of a dollar. I just need you to subtly look at the faces of the people around and see if you get anything... please,' he added.

'Sure. I might have had more luck in the shopping centre.'

Murdoch glanced her way. 'I'm happy to take you there after if you have the time.'

She nodded and studied the neighbourhood as Murdoch pulled into a quiet street and parked at the end of the driveway of a large home. There was a high fence around the yard, a swing visible through the fence bars, and numerous cars around the road. No media vans yet.

'Hope they are all just friends and family,' he muttered on seeing the people lingering at the other end of the driveway, closer to the front door of the residence. 'I'll introduce you as a consultant if that's okay?' He cut the engine.

'Fine. I'll just slip into a corner and see what I can detect. Nice area, a bit of money around here,' Sophie said. They alighted from the car and began the long walk up the driveway. Murdoch adjusted his tie and Sophie did her best to match his step and keep up.

'I believe the family made their money in herbal products – shampoos, soaps, good smelling stuff,' Murdoch said quietly. 'They've recently moved into eco-clothing or some bloody thing.'

Sophie tried not to laugh at Murdoch's summary, given the solemness of the situation.

Murdoch continued: 'They might have made an enemy or two among competitors; I'm yet to explore that. But I know they've been splashing a lot of money on advertising where they are promoted as the hottest and healthiest pair around wearing their eco-gear, looking sparkling and healthy.'

'Ah envy and greed, two good motives no doubt?' Sophie asked and Murdoch grunted his agreement. She stopped while she took her glasses – the pair that made her what she was – from her handbag.

'Sorry,' she apologised for making Murdoch wait. 'There are so many people hanging around, I should start reading earlier than later.'

He accepted her need to wear the glasses – Daphne, her

great aunt whom he worked with and solved many cases with over the years, was the same.

'I need the glasses to see people's features in order to read them,' she mumbled by way of explanation. She offered the excuse every time she put them on. It would be easier if she wore glasses all the time, and then it wouldn't seem so odd.

They continued their walk up the driveway. An older couple was coming towards them. They greeted Murdoch and Sophie. The older man was supporting the woman, while she dabbed her eyes with a handkerchief.

'Are you related to the family?' Murdoch asked after greeting them.

'Grandparents, paternal side,' the elderly gentleman said. 'It's too distressing for my wife's health to remain.'

'Of course,' Murdoch said and glanced at Sophie.

She shook her head. They were not involved, as they both expected. Murdoch allowed them to continue walking past. Two junior constables approached.

'I don't want people coming and going,' Murdoch told them. 'No one else in or out for now.'

'Yes sir,' one of the uniformed men said. 'We'll position ourselves at the entrance gates.'

Sophie watched them head to the gates. She saw one officer was going to leave the force with an injury. She didn't have time to read the other.

Murdoch and Sophie continued up the path as two young men came down towards them. Sophie had to stop each time; it was hard walking with the glasses on. She would have to get Alfred, Lukas or Orli – her partners in the curse's history – that is, gift – to make a set of glasses for her that allowed for more movement.

'We're asking people not to leave, sorry guys,' Murdoch stopped the two young men. They were in their late teens, dressed in jeans, with black T-shirts and caps.

'We've got to get to work,' one of them said.

'Are you related to the Kingsley family?' Murdoch asked.

'I'm a nephew, this is my best friend. We came to see if we could do anything.'

'How did you hear about it?' Sophie asked, surprising Murdoch. She needed specific questions to be asked to see the big picture, to receive the images from the glasses, and to generate the visions they needed to solve this case. Different images of the two young men appeared around her and changed as they responded to her question.

'We ran into my aunt up the road at the shopping centre. It had just happened, she was freaking out,' he said.

'And you saw nothing?' Murdoch asked.

Both men shook their heads.

'Alright then,' Murdoch said and relented, moving them on with a wave of his hand. The two men hurried off.

Sophie grabbed his arm and he looked toward her. She was staring at the nephew, her look intent.

'He has the little girl. She's in the boot of his car. Ransom… he's going to ask for a ransom.'

'What?' Murdoch asked, shocked, and turned towards them.

'The little girl was holding their hands, smiling, and they've got her now, here. She's alive.'

'Hey, wait up!' he called, running after them. Murdoch yelled to his two constables to stop the men. The nephew turned at the sound of the yelling and saw Murdoch in pursuit.

'Run!' he yelled at his mate and they broke into a sprint.

Sophie watched it all unfold like a movie, some of which she'd seen with her glasses.

'Stop them,' Murdoch yelled, closing the distance between himself and the young men.

The constables closed the gates as the nephew and his friend ran at them.

'Get out of the way!' the nephew yelled.

His friend threw himself up onto the top of the fence and a constable grabbed him around the ankles, pulling him down. A large man ran towards them and Murdoch braced, expecting to be hit, but he helped the detective instead.

'Friend of the family,' he explained, as he helped the constable restrain the nephew's mate.

Murdoch slammed the nephew against the fence, while the second constable cuffed him.

'Where are your keys?' he demanded.

The nephew spat at him, and Murdoch rolled his eyes and wiped the spit with his shirt sleeve. The constable patted the nephew's pockets and retrieved them.

'Here you are, Sir.'

Murdoch nodded his thanks and glanced around to find Sophie was now nearby.

'It's the blue car that I saw,' she said and pointed to a sports car with thick wheels. 'That's it, I think.'

Murdoch hit the unlock button on the set of keys, and the car beeped. With Sophie, they raced to the vehicle, opened the boot and there she lay, the little girl, frightened, wide-eyed, looking up at them.

'You're okay, darling, we're the police,' Murdoch said,

and a constable arrived at his side in uniform. She raised her arms and allowed Murdoch to lift her out of the car, and Sophie watched as he walked up the path, holding her close. He looked rather gorgeous, Sophie conceded, manly and strong, as he carried the little child as if she were his daughter. The cries of relief and jubilation at the sight of the lost child brought her parents running from the house. They gratefully took her from Murdoch's arms; the family crying and hugging each other.

Sophia glanced at her watch. If she called a taxi, she might just make that audition after all.

Chapter 2

In winter, the afternoon was the best time of the day to visit the *Optical Illusion* store – the sunlight hit the little shop at approximately one-thirty p.m., making it gleam like a crystal wonderland with its leadlight windows, rich mahogany timber-framed entrance, and diamond-shaped glass panel. Assuming, of course, you could find the tiny store wedged between *The Perfect Slice* cake store and *Just the Thing* gift emporium.

This afternoon, Mr Alfred Lens was polishing the crystal figurines – one of the store's best-selling items. His father apprenticed Alfred into the business as a young man. Now Alfred was the proud owner. Nearing seventy, he still lived upstairs, in the residence he grew up in with his parents and siblings above the store. Retirement was joked about but never seriously discussed. After all, Alfred, his grandson, Lukas Lens, and niece, Orli, all had their speciality areas and complemented each other perfectly in the business.

Working, sitting on a chair at the opposite bench was

handsome, tall and mysterious, Lukas Lens, 25, a master clocksmith. He brushed back the light brown hair that had fallen across his eyes as he worked on an antique clock and lifted his pale blue eyes to his grandfather.

'You're reading me,' he said, touching his temple lightly where he felt the buzz of his grandfather's intrusion in his mind.

'Am I?' his grandfather asked, surprised, as he looked up from his work. 'It was not intentional. I was, however, thinking about you.'

'I'm hesitant to ask, but what were you thinking?' Lukas said with a smile to his grandfather, who chuckled.

'I'll think it again, and you try to read me,' Alfred suggested.

'It's your gift, not mine. I don't think it will be one I will master,' Lukas said, a hint of frustration in his voice. He desperately wanted that gift, but instead, the bloodline had given him other bounties. 'It would be really helpful if I could read Sophie, given I am her protector.'

Alfred nodded. 'It was immensely helpful to me when I was required to protect Daphne, God rest her soul. You have been improving, keep it up,' he encouraged his grandson. 'I am thinking about it now, try.'

Lukas nodded. He kept working as he tried to hear his grandfather's thoughts, but could not get a word.

Alfred knew Lukas wasn't succeeding; he couldn't feel Lukas's intrusion in his mind. He changed his thought to something light and simple. Soon, he felt the familiar buzz of intrusion.

Lukas stopped working, closed his eyes, and concentrated harder. Then he burst out laughing.

'If you like,' he said, and his grandfather grinned.

'Well done, my boy. And I really do want my ashes put in a crystal urn and placed on the highest ledge. I can keep an eye on you then.'

Lukas shook his head. 'You'll still be reading me.' He sobered. 'But you haven't fooled me, Grandpa… you weren't thinking that or you wouldn't have been in my head.'

'That's true,' Alfred conceded. 'The raven is near Sophie and you are worried.'

'Yes.'

'He likes her, this might be different…'

'It never has been since the history of time,' Lukas said.

'No,' Alfred conceded. They thought about that for some time in silence. Then Alfred looked to the door: 'Oh, here is Lucy,' he said, with a smile, shelving the discussion as Lukas's girlfriend of a few months appeared outside.

The quaint silver bell which sat above the door tinkled as Lucy entered. Both men greeted her with delight, but Alfred excused himself to check some stock out the back, leaving the young pair alone.

Alfred knew something wasn't right between the couple, but couldn't decipher it yet. He wasn't sure Lukas could either, from what he read on his grandson's mind this afternoon, but there was something brewing. He thought about Miss Sharpe whom he had always held a deep affection for, loved if he was to be open and honest. She had said Sophie would be the most powerful clairvoyant of her time, of the cursed line. He had his suspicions why, and while there was nothing he could do about it, he wanted to be sure his grandson was safe. He had raised the boy since he was a teenager. Alfred needed to speak with Orli, his niece, to see if she knew what was brewing. This was a matter for her more spiritually connected mind.

Chapter 3

Sophie tiptoed into the darkened stage area and quietly sat next to another woman of similar age but darker colouring. They smiled a greeting to each other and returned their attention to the current audition on stage. Sophie made it on time, twenty minutes to spare, and strangely, she felt better for it... not having a long sitting period before the audition gave her less time to be nervous. She was running on adrenaline instead. The play was an original script; the director was well respected and Sophie wanted to come to his notice. The choice of audition script was up to the actor for the first round, but a call back would no doubt require the actors to learn a scene from the new play.

On stage, the actress was doing an impressive portrayal of a scene from *Cat on a Hot Tin Roof*. Too good, Sophie thought with a frown. *Whatever.* Then she realised what she had just said to herself. Something had shifted. Her hunger to do the audition, to win the role, was not there. Was this some kind of rub off from the glasses? She didn't notice the actress on stage had finished and the lady next to her had risen for her audition.

'Best of luck,' Sophie called after her just in time and she turned to thank her. The actress had that look Sophie recognised as quiet desperation. She wasn't feeling it. In fact, she wasn't sure that she had time to be learning lines and performing twice a day with a matinee and evening show. Sophie rose and did something she never thought she would. She departed.

*****

'Well, aren't you the clever clog?' Miss Sharpe beamed at her as she returned to the office, or rather the huge rambling estate of her aunt where Sophie now had her office.

Sophie laughed, regarding the neat and extremely efficient Miss Sharpe with affection. Miss Sharpe had come with the glasses – bequeathed by Aunt Daphne – like a package deal. Tall and wiry like a glasses frame, she fitted her name and was unerringly loyal having served Bertram Lens as a very young typist, then after falling in love with Bertram's son, Alfred Lens – and deeming that situation unprofessional – she transferred her services to Aunt Daphne. What a pair they were for decades.

Neither Miss Sharpe nor Sophie expected they could work together, or even like each other, but that was fast-changing. Miss Sharpe was enjoying the energy of the young woman and Sophie's journey of discovery and compassion. Sophie had told Miss Sharpe straight up she could not do what was required without her. Now they had become a formidable team.

'We did it! Did Murdoch tell you already?' Sophie asked, surprised.

'It's all over the internet,' Miss Sharpe said. 'Plus, you have been lauded. I had to put the answering machine on for a while to manage the interview requests and appointments coming in.'

Sophie laughed, delighted. 'Good idea. There's only so many we can do.'

'The nephew, what a terrible thing,' Miss Sharpe sighed. 'They are saying online that he had been planning it for some time and expected to grab the money and have his little cousin back by the next day, no one the wiser.'

'After causing all that fear and distress,' Sophie said and shook her head. 'He almost got away from us too. I didn't put the glasses on early enough.'

'Goodness!' Miss Sharpe exclaimed. 'Did you make the audition?'

'Yes. And no,' Sophie said, and happily accepted the offer of a cup of tea from the pot Miss Sharpe had just brewed. 'A funny thing happened when I was at the audition... but you knew that, of course.'

Miss Sharpe smiled. 'Perhaps.'

'I suspect you know quite a bit about my future, Miss Sharpe,' Sophie teased. 'Just how much did Aunt Daphne tell you?'

The ladies sat down with their tea and a small plate of Miss Sharpe's shortbread biscuits and Miss Sharpe responded: 'Enough to know that you would make a difference, my dear, and I am thrilled that you have already done so. Incidentally, Orli rang, she said you might want some new frames for the glasses.'

Sophie shook her head. 'I swear Miss Sharpe, between

yourself and the Lens family, I am not sure I am the one who has the psychic skills. If it weren't for the glasses…'

'But it is more than that, isn't it, dear?' Miss Sharpe said. 'The glasses let you see futures, but the line you come from, well, it is a powerful line and only one descendant per generation has the gift.'

Sophie frowned. 'But I'm nothing without the glasses. I have no skills. Whereas, Alfred, Lukas and Orli – even Murdoch – are descendants of the witch, Saghani. Like her, they have powers, just as she had the power to curse my family with the sightings when we wore glasses. I know it was a long time ago…'

'In the year of 1582,' Miss Sharpe said, having read the family history books and retained the detail with her sharp mind.

'Exactly, but my line was not gifted, were they? We were the ones that looked a gift horse in the mouth and had Saghani killed for being a witch,' Sophie scoffed. 'I am the most vulnerable of them all.' She sighed with frustration.

Miss Sharpe pursed her lips.

'Ah, ha, I know that look Miss Sharpe, you're trying not to tell me something.'

Miss Sharpe smiled. 'It's not so much that, Sophie, dear. It's just that you have come so far in so little time and handled this transition beautifully. I'm hesitant to overload you when you are not finished reading the family history yet and won't for some time.'

'But Alfred said I could read it out of order and there are things I should know, that I should jump ahead to, like the raven. I have more power knowing who the enemy is that wreaked havoc on some of my descendants – well, the enemy of my generation.'

'Yes, I agree with Alfred that it is wise to do that.'

'But now you are implying that there is witchery on my side of the family too?' Sophie asked.

Miss Sharpe conceded the point. 'It is part of the reason your distant relative acted with such vengeance when Saghani cured him with what he believed was witchcraft – he had experience of it in his own family line... your family line. Fear is a powerful motivator for extremes of behaviour.'

Sophie nodded, sipped her tea and thought. 'So, if I am to understand this, we had powers too, and did he not want it known so he thought punishing another witch would take the spotlight from him, or did he have a bad experience with witchery?'

'I don't like to spoil the story for you,' Miss Sharpe said with a small smile. 'But you are on the right path with both assumptions.'

'This is exciting,' Sophie said, her eyes widening with the promise of the powers she might possess.

'You need to be very cautious, dear.'

'Yes,' Sophie said, reining in her enthusiasm at seeing Miss Sharpe's concerned look.

'I think it is best you talk to Lukas about it.'

'Not Alfred?' Sophie asked, surprised, and Miss Sharpe shook her head.

'No, Lukas is your protector now. You should learn and move forward together. It will make you a stronger coupling.'

'I must remember he is learning too, and try and be more understanding when he is reticent about my requests, and he has been in some instances.'

'He would not be doing his job if he wasn't,' Miss Sharpe pointed out.

They sat for a few moments drinking their tea and then Miss Sharpe asked: 'How did you feel with Murdoch this morning, now that you know?'

Sophie bit her lower lip as she thought. 'It was awkward for me, at first, but I don't think Murdoch sensed I was worried or watching him. I can't believe he is a raven descendant.'

'Could have knocked me over with a feather too,' Miss Sharpe said.

'A raven feather?' Sophie asked and made her laugh.

'He is very different to the other side of his family line – Lukas and Orli – at least physically,' Miss Sharpe said.

'Yes, and in nature. He is moodier. If I had to line up fifty people in my lifetime, my generation, that I thought might be my enemy from the cursed line, Murdoch would not be on that line-up. He's so...'

'Gentlemanly, kind, likeable...' Miss Sharpe offered.

'No, none of those things,' Sophie said, and with a glance at Miss Sharpe, they both laughed. 'He may be those things with you, but I rarely see them. But he is a detective... he defends and protects. He has a compass pointing to good, not evil. I like him.'

'And he likes you.'

'But if he knew about the curse and our bloodlines, if he knew he was the raven to Lukas's dove, that I am from his enemy line, could he still like me?' Sophie asked. 'If he never finds out, then we may continue as we are, I guess. Or, he might even think it is a load of rubbish,' she said, thinking aloud.

'Maybe you would have thought the power of the glasses was rubbish too, Sophie, if you had not seen with your own eyes. Would you not?' Miss Sharpe asked.

Sophie nodded. 'Yes, true.'

'Knowledge is power, my dear. Perhaps you are right. Perhaps you need to read as much as you can about your own line, and be ready for whatever might come your way.'

Sophie finished her tea and, picking up another biscuit, asked: 'Permission to be excused Miss Sharpe, and I shall go visit *Optical Illusion.*'

Miss Sharpe chuckled. 'Permission granted. You have no bookings today as I assumed you would be at the audition.'

'Did you really?' Sophie teased.

'Well, I assumed you would be busy, especially with the media interviews,' Miss Sharpe said with a sly look. 'Do go and read some more of your family history while you have a window of availability. With the calls coming through, you are going to be very busy and you have three readings tomorrow.'

Sophie thanked Miss Sharpe, and rose, departing to ask Lukas about her witching history and read more of the book that was protected under lock and key by the guardians of her family history, Alfred, Lukas and Orli Lens.

Chapter 4

'Are you going to involve her in every case we have from now on?' Detective Gerard Oakley grumbled.

Murdoch was used to his partner, who, on a good day was grumpy at best. Today was like every other.

'It hasn't hurt our stats, has it? We've now solved more cases than any other partnership thanks to Daphne, and now two cases closed with Sophie's help and she's just beginning,' Murdoch said, with a glance to Gerard before returning his attention to the road and driving. 'People might even think you and I get on since we're so successful.'

Gerard chuckled. 'Lord help us.'

'And no, I don't intend to involve her all the time. But when a kid is missing and time is crucial, I'd be stupid not to come in guns blazing.'

'Fair enough,' Gerard said. They sat in silence for a few moments before Gerard started up again. He never could stand silence. 'She's a looker, I'll give you that much. I'd do her.'

Murdoch grimaced at his partner's disrespect, which he wrote off as boy-club thinking. The thought of his older, stocky, weathered partner *doing* Sophie wasn't a vision he wanted in his head.

'Yeah, you'd be just her type,' he deadpanned, and got another laugh from Gerard. Murdoch ran a hand over his chin and wondered what Sophie thought of him, if she thought of him at all. The first case he worked with her involved Murdoch's ex-fiancé, and he was devastated by the outcome. His heart was only just on the mend.

Gerard talked on. 'She'll be in demand soon and every cop will be asking for her help. You'll probably be lucky if she has time to see you.' His comment riled Murdoch. He didn't want to think of Sophie partnering with every other cop in town, but now that Gerard had put the thought in his mind, it annoyed him how much that bothered him. He and Sophie hadn't had the best of starts, but he was working on being more open, a bit more sympathetic to what she did, and if he could manage it, a bit more charming. It didn't come easy when she had attitude to spare.

Murdoch realised Gerard was still talking. He was tempted to turn the car radio up and block him out.

'There's one cold case that haunts me,' Gerard said. 'I'd love to solve it before I retire next year. It'd be great to never think about it again.'

Now he had Murdoch's interest.

'Which case? Tell me about it?' Murdoch encouraged him, and it took the focus off Sophie for now.

'Before your time,' Gerard said. 'I was in my early thirties; about the age you are now. I'd been partnered with some old bastard, a bit like you getting stuck with me, only you're lucky. I'm easy-going.'

Murdoch scoffed. 'Yeah, well you wait long enough, everything comes back around to bite you.'

'Ain't that the truth,' Gerard smirked. 'I was trying to prove myself, and my partner, Frank, didn't give a toss about much except getting to the weekend and fishing. But I kid you not, this case kept me awake at night for years – Cassie Delaney.'

'Can't say I remember that one,' Murdoch said.

'Well, you wouldn't. It was three decades ago and you would have been a brat in arms,' Gerard said, smiling at his own play on words.

Murdoch turned into their car parking lot, disappointed they had not started this conversation earlier.

'So, what's Cassie's story?' he asked, directing his partner to cut to the chase.

'She was the carnival beauty queen, a trainee teacher, had a boyfriend who played in a band, parents and friends that adored her... and the night of her 21st birthday she went missing, a little after 11pm,' Gerard said. 'Most beautiful girl I'd ever seen, she was. We found her behind the wheel of her car at the bottom of the creek near her home. She'd won the car in the beauty quest. Cassie had died of a drug overdose, not from drowning, but she wasn't a drug user and no one saw what happened to her.'

Murdoch cut the ignition and paused before opening the door.

'How long until she was found?'

'About a week after she went missing. Initially, we thought she left with a man, someone who caught her eye at the party. But how she ended up at the bottom of the creek at the wheel of her own car remains a mystery.'

The men alighted and headed into work.

'Wow, that sounds like someone really had it in for her,' Murdoch said. 'Maybe Sophie can solve that one for you, let you retire in peace.'

Gerard shrugged. 'I might just let her.'

'Yeah, well if you put it to her like that, I can tell you what she'll say and it won't be yes.'

Gerard grinned. 'Why don't you ask her for me? It'll give you another chance to visit her.'

'I'm not looking for—' Murdoch stopped, realising his partner was baiting him.

'Sure you're not,' Gerard said with a sly look. 'You need to get back on the horse.'

'Yep,' Murdoch said, agreeing to shut his partner down.

'Age before beauty,' Gerard muttered as he opened the door and barged into the building ahead of his partner.

Chapter 5

It was just nearing 2pm when Sophie found herself a parking spot and arrived at the door of *Optical Illusion*. A comfortable post-lunch lull had descended on the street. Window shopping, the morning rush, and lunchtime browsing had concluded. The *Optical Illusion* shop, for one, was in a state of comfortableness.

Sophie could see through the window that Alfred was by himself behind the counter, sitting on a stool and reading what looked to be an industry magazine. He looked impressively formal in his dark suit, with this thinning silver hair and thin silver-rimmed glasses. Sophie had the chance to study him momentarily before she opened the door. It felt like she had stepped back in time, into a small store in the laneways of London. She expected to look around her and see cobblestones on the road.

Entering the shop, the bell tinkled above her; Alfred looked up and smiled with delight.

'Well, this is a lovely surprise. Welcome Sophie,' he stood to greet her.

'Alfred, the pleasure is all mine,' she said with a small curtsy and made him laugh with her old-fashioned charm. 'The shop brings it out in me.'

'Then it is working,' he said, pleased. 'It was our intention to create a little place of respite where one could feel charmed and safe.'

Sophie accepted Alfred's invitation and sat on one of the small stools on the opposite side of the counter to him, usually occupied by customers wanting jewellery fittings.

'Are you sailing the ship alone?' she asked.

'Yes, the captain's work is never done,' Alfred said with a shake of his head. 'Present company excepted, I do like a bit of quiet time though, I confess.'

'I wish I did,' Sophie said. 'I find if I am not distracted that I am thinking too much, and that is quite exhausting. There seems to be so much to learn and think about at the moment.'

'In your case, that is very true,' Alfred agreed.

He asked after Miss Sharpe's health and then the bell rang behind them and Orli entered – Alfred's ethereal niece and the store's qualified optometrist. Unlike her uncle, Alfred, who was apprenticed by his father, Bertram, Orli did her optometry qualification at university and these days managed all the store's clients. Alfred had long since stopped looking into people's eyes for professional purposes.

Sophie found it hard to tear her gaze from Orli – willowy of appearance and with her name meaning 'light', Orli radiated it. Despite being only 22 years of age, Orli's hair was white, her features pale, and she shared the lightest of blue eyes that ran in Alfred and Lukas's family.

'Sophie! I was hoping to catch you,' she said, her voice musical. 'I have several frames for you to consider. It's time you made the glasses your own!'

Sophie rose and the two ladies hugged.

'Yes, please,' Sophie said. 'Aunt Daphne's very serious dark frames make me look like a cranky matron, and I confess I can't walk and read people at the same time without falling over.'

Alfred chuckled. 'Neither can I and I have no excuse.'

The two ladies laughed and looked at him with great affection.

'We can fix that Sophie. As for you, Uncle Alfred, you're a lost cause,' Orli teased him and he laughed. She turned back to Sophie. 'We'll improve the glass in the lower half of your pair and see if that helps with walking and your balance. Drop into the backroom and see me before you go and I'll give you the sample frames I've set aside for you. You can try them on at home.'

'Ooh, that'll be perfect thank you, I can take them on and off a thousand times and not worry I'm holding you up,' Sophie said.

The bell rang again and Lukas and Lucy entered. Sophie smiled with delight on seeing them.

'We've been to lunch,' Lucy told Sophie, 'I thought I'd better get Lukas back to work in case he gets in trouble.'

'Yes, the boss is a terrible taskmaster,' Lukas joked with a smile to his grandfather. 'It's good to see you Sophie, congratulations, what a great outcome.'

Everyone joined in and she thanked them modestly, telling them again how she nearly did not catch the nephew.

'You've come to read, I imagine,' Lukas said and Sophie nodded. 'I'll see Lucy out and get you started.'

'I'll get the book,' Alfred said and Sophie took her usual spot by the desk. She gave Lucy a quick wave and said she would see her tonight but she sensed something was wrong, and that was without the glasses.

*****

Sophie accepted the book and opened it, she glanced at the entries and decided to read a short one while she waited for Lukas to return. She was after a very specific entry today or at least some information about her witching powers and ancestry. She turned the pages and found a brief entry that grabbed her attention.

The history of the glasses
The reign of Grace Waterson – 4 March, 1888

(Note to book beholder: translated from the traditional word to modern speak by Alfred Lens, 13 May, 1981)

It was not my intent, but I have fallen in love. Love is a grand thing and for so long I had wished to lose my heart and my hand to a husband of choice, but my heart has chosen one that it should not – my protector, James. He is a fine, tall man, handsome of features with the lightest blue eyes that transfix me with one glance. He is kind and a gentleman in every sense. A protector relationship is not forbidden, nor discouraged. Owners of the curse before me have partnered with their protectors and in most cases lived happily together, but my protector has another. He is betrothed to Lily and he loves her, but not with the passion we share and it has not been without its difficulties since we were partnered.

They became engaged some three years earlier, a rash, youthful promise made in the first glow of love, before he took to the sea for two years. Lily dutifully waited, and on his return, they resumed their relationship both a little older and wiser. He has informed me that their pairing was not as dear as it once was, to either of them. However, Lily has waited for him for two years and deserves the obligation to be met. I am not one to trifle with anyone's affections.

James has told me that Lily does not like his connection to me or understands our friendship. I have not seen Lily so I cannot read if they are to marry. I cannot read my protector, nor could any of the curse holders in our history, so my heart is open to the possibility that we may find ourselves together. What torture to see him so often and to know he returns to someone else. Might I have to seek another protector? Would he be willing to let me go for both of our sakes?

*****

Sophie stopped reading. Hmm, tough one, she thought. She could easily imagine how the curse carriers, herself included, could fall for their protectors. If she had not been so dismissive initially of Daphne's gifted glasses and almost not collected them, her first encounter with Lukas would have been different, instead of rushed and disinterested. He met her friend Lucy, and the rest was history.

Speaking of which, the bell tinkled and Lukas re-entered the store. He looked strikingly handsome; it ran in the Lens' family. Sophie realised Grace's description of her protector, James, in the late 19th century could equally apply to Lukas. He shuffled his jacket on and, while he didn't wear a tie like his grandfather, he looked well dressed for behind the counter.

'Sorry,' he said with a smile in her direction.

'No apology necessary,' Sophie assured him. 'I was reading one of Grace Waterson's accounts. The one where she found love.'

'I don't recall Grace, but there are so many and I don't have a photographic memory,' he said with a glance to Alfred, testing him. 'What was Grace's story, Grandpa, I bet you remember?'

'Wasn't she one of the ladies who fell in love with her protector?' Alfred asked.

'Yes, James, but I've just read he was betrothed to Lily.'

'Ah yes, that Grace. I'm afraid she met a gruesome end,' Alfred said. 'Do you want me to spoil the ending and tell you?'

Sophie grimaced, 'You will have to now and put us out of our misery.'

Lukas smiled at her until Alfred pronounced: 'Grace was poisoned.'

'No!' Sophie exclaimed.

Lukas sat down on a customer stool. 'I didn't see that coming. So who did it?'

'James's fiancée. Poor dear Grace died, and they hanged Lily,' Alfred said. 'Sorry to deliver such ghastly news.'

'Good grief,' Sophie exclaimed. 'There's more danger than I thought involved in this "seeing visions" business!'

'So true. The eyes are the window to the soul, after all,' Alfred said and rising, he excused himself to speak with Orli in the room behind the showroom.

Sophie turned to Lukas. 'I hope Lucy doesn't decide to bump me off and then go to prison for it,' she joked.

'I don't think she is too worried about you and me,' Lukas assured Sophie.

'Of course not. Why would she be worried when she is gorgeous... why would you look at me?' Sophie said, feeling the sting of his words.

'I didn't mean it to come out like that,' he hurriedly assured her. 'Sorry, that's not what I meant, I assure you.' Lukas stumbled over the words.

Sophie smiled. 'That's okay, we're new at this, we're bound to stand on each other's toes a bit.'

He gave her a nod of agreement and changed the subject. 'I sense you are here for more than a reading.'

She nodded. 'I'm ready for the next phase.'

He looked surprised and then frowned. 'Uh oh, what phase is that.'

'The witchery.'

Lukas visibly relaxed. 'Right, the witchery. So do you want to know more about Hadley's side of the family, that is, our side – the doves,' he clarified, 'or Harley's lot... the ravens?'

'Neither. I want to know about the witchery on *my* side of the family.'

Lukas paused; his eyes narrowed.

'I know you don't want to tell me, and I know you don't think I am ready…' Sophie challenged him, 'but Lukas, I have to know things when I want to know them, otherwise, it will be all I will think about and it will distract me.'

Lukas looked displeased. 'Daphne did not want you to know about this until you had your powers for a few years at least,' he said firmly. 'There is a timeline that Alfred and Daphne worked to and I've now got to implement.'

Sophie rolled her eyes. 'I am not Aunt Daphne. She's gone and my skills are different to hers, my needs are different.'

Lukas glanced towards the back of the showroom. Sophie could understand he was torn between consulting with his grandfather and making decisions now on his own that were best for her.

He cleared his throat and said in a very rational voice. 'My concern is that we may have too much to deal with too soon before we are used to working together and, like you said, before we've worked out your needs and mine as your protector. It's only been a few months, and I'd rather wait.'

'I don't understand why I have to ask permission to find out information!' Sophie snapped with frustration. 'If it is written somewhere, you can just direct me there and I'll read it without you getting involved, if you prefer.'

'Great, thanks Sophie. I'll just be at your call when needed then.'

They glared at each other.

Lukas tried again. 'I don't understand what the rush is, you don't even know what you are capable of doing yet with the glasses.'

Sophie did her best to rein in her impatience, remembering what Miss Sharpe said about Lukas doing his job. 'I know this – what you are doing now – is trying to protect me, Lukas, and I appreciate that. But Miss Sharpe thinks I am ready for it as well, so why do you think I'm such an idiot?'

He rolled his eyes and looked away before answering: 'I don't think you are an idiot. Why can't you trust me, that I'm doing what is best for both of us?'

The question surprised Sophie, and when she didn't immediately answer he turned to look at her.

'Why don't you trust I know what is best for me?' she asked.

'What do you want the powers for?'

'Nothing. I'm not seeking power, I'm seeking understanding. I'm not looking to do anything with the information other than being better informed.' She sighed. 'I just want to know what I am capable of so that if I need to protect myself, I can.'

'That's my job.'

'And you are going to be there every hour of every day?'

'Yes.'

'Well, we just saw how well that went for Grace who was poisoned. I don't think Lucy will be happy if you are at my beck and call.' She shook her head in disbelief.

The air was crackling with tension as they glared at each other. Lukas's pale eyes trying to read her deeper blue eyes; Sophie steadfast in her stubbornness making her even more strong and beautiful.

In a controlled voice, Sophie explained: 'I want to know

because everyone else does in this family. You all know more about me than I know about me. It is my right.'

'You don't have any rights, Sophie. This began because your ancestor killed mine in cold blood.'

Sophie rose and snapped the book closed. 'Wow! Really Lukas? Why bother protecting our line then? Hang up your cape!'

Her eyes widened as Lukas's eyes flared yellow with anger.

A force of pure energy knocked Sophie to the floor and the large crystal urn behind Lukas, that Alfred intended to put his ashes in, shattered sending slivers of glass raining down on the two inhabitants of the room.

Chapter 6

The shattering of glass sounded like a gunshot. Sophie cried out in surprise and fright as she hit the floor, crystal and glass shattering around her. Lukas was beside her in a flash, sheltering her from the shards. From nowhere, Orli and Alfred appeared instantly in the room as if they had transcended from the back room.

Lukas froze, his senses completely heightened to the degree he could hear the glass crystals shattering as each piece hit the floor. He felt everything happening around him in slow motion. Through narrowed eyes he saw Orli raise Sophie from the floor, pulling her away from Lukas and bundling her outside the store saying the words: 'Forgive us, Sophie. Please go, we'll be in contact as soon as we can.' He saw his grandfather lock the shop door and reverse the closed sign.

Lukas stood like an evangelist in his dark suit in the middle of the room, strong and resolute. His arms away from his body, legs apart – a vessel for the rush of anger, the power in his hands, extreme vision in his gold eyes – as

Orli scrambled to harness his anger. He felt his grandfather creating a protective shield around him, and now Alfred was in his head, saying calming words, trying to focus him. For an older man, Alfred was strong, spiritually and mentally. Lukas felt his grandfather's hands on his shoulders and his grandfather's orders in his head, stepping him back out of the room filled with glass into the backroom. Lukas did his best not to touch the surfaces that he would destroy instantly. His vision was as if he were wearing a night lens – everything was gold, and fast and angular. Despite the noise in his head, the shakes in his body, tingling in his hands and distorted vision, guided by Alfred, he made it through to the backroom and slumped against a wall. Lukas felt like he had been struck by lightning.

Released by Alfred, he raised his hands, webbing his fingers behind his head and sliding down the wall, slumped to the floor. Orli rushed in and squatted beside him. She placed her fingers on his temple and saw him wince.

'Sorry,' she whispered and chanted until he was still, until it was quiet, and there were no tremors left in his body.

Eventually, Lukas opened his eyes and his vision was back to normal. Orli rose and studied him; his grandfather stood nearby. Alfred moved away, poured several glasses of water and the three witches replenished and said nothing for just a moment, to regroup. Alfred pulled a chair away from Orli's desk and sat.

Lukas shook his head. 'I'm sorry,' he said and swallowed. 'She made me angry.'

Orli gave an uncharacteristic giggle, and they looked at her. She shrugged. 'It was a bit of an understatement.'

Alfred smiled and with the tension gone, the three of them all shared a small laugh. When they sobered, Alfred said: 'Lukas, I'm not sure it is going to work, you and Sophie.'

'Nor am I,' Orli said rising and seating herself next to Alfred as he pulled a chair out for her.

Lukas groaned and extended his legs in front of him. 'Don't give up on us yet. I'll work on it; I'll work at being calmer. I'm sorry about the damage.'

'I can fix it, don't be concerned,' Orli said.

Alfred sighed. 'It's been a long time since you've had this level of rage... since...' he hesitated.

'Since Mum and Dad died,' Lukas said finishing his sentence. 'I didn't know why then,' he said, realisation sinking in. 'I didn't know it was inherited, I just thought I was so angry at the way they died.'

'You can still learn to control it regardless of it being inherited,' Alfred said, 'look at Orli.'

'Look at you, Uncle!' Orli said, 'you are the calmest man I have ever met.'

'Great,' Lukas mumbled. 'It's just me then.'

The three all shared another smile.

'I need to apologise to Sophie,' Lukas said, brushing glass off his shoulders.

'Leave it until tomorrow maybe,' Orli suggested.

'To give her time to calm down too?' Lukas asked.

'No. I think you frightened her,' Orli said and Lukas looked ashamed.

'Maybe you are right, Grandpa. Maybe I am not the best one to be her protector.'

Alfred placed his hands on his knees as if decreeing

the next action. 'Orli and I will talk with Miss Sharpe and see how she feels and what she has gleaned from Sophie. Perhaps you better take up boxing or something to channel your anger, Lukas.'

'That's actually not a bad idea,' he said. He rose and pulled a chair away from the table, and sat as well, reaching for his glass of water.

Orli studied him. 'But seriously Lukas, you need anger channelling and I think you should start lessons soon,' she said with a look to Alfred who nodded his agreement.

Lukas narrowed his eyes. 'What does that involve?'

'You face your contenders who teach you how to channel your anger because if you don't, what they are sending your way will hurt you,' Orli said and bit her lip.

Alfred huffed remembering it. 'Trust me, as soon as you receive a few bursts of pain, you either roll into a ball or get angry. Those that get angry – and I suspect you will be that type, my boy – will react.'

'You will get hurt but at the end, you'll be stronger and better for it, and safer around others,' Orli said.

Lukas looked from one to the other. 'Have either of you been through it as a teacher or subject?'

Alfred nodded. 'Both, and Orli teaches.'

Lukas laughed. 'I can't imagine either of you getting angry enough to hurt someone.'

'See, it works,' Alfred said and smiled. 'My father did it for my brothers and me. He was powerful, it took me a few months to recover I took such a beating.'

'Didn't he feel bad?' Lukas asked shocked.

'He felt responsible. If my brothers or I had hurt or killed anyone because we could not manage our power, then our lives would be over, as would the victim's. He did it out of love, and he was right to do so. I did the same with my son.'

Lukas's eyes widened with surprise. 'Dad did anger channelling?'

'He was a talented student but not quick to anger like I was at his age, so it was a much more pleasant experience than I had with your great-grandfather. I guess I was waiting to see if you took after me or your father to see if you needed it.'

Lukas thought about it for a moment until Orli interrupted his thoughts.

'Alfred is the strongest of the three of us, he could manage you best,' she said and Lukas shook his head.

'Absolutely no way. If you think I'm going to risk doing that with you, Grandpa, you're both tripping. When you were younger maybe.'

Alfred smiled at him. 'My physical age does not bear on my spiritual strength, you need not be concerned you could harm me, even when we get to the point where you can channel successfully.'

Orli nodded her head in agreement as Lukas studied them both. He rose from his chair and looked through the door to the showroom and the damage he caused.

'No, I don't want to risk it,' he said.

Suddenly Lukas was hauled backward, flipped over, and pushed to the floor, a weight on his back pressing him down. He struggled and could not rise. He could see Alfred and Orli remained seated where they were.

'What the hell…' he hissed with the pain and pressure

keeping him down. He fought, trying to rise, his anger and humiliation burning.

'Try harder,' Alfred said.

Lukas struggled, pushing with a yell of anger, then he slumped, spent. He glanced up at Alfred who had not moved, except to straighten his tie.

'Let me know if you change your mind, lad,' he said and rising, he offered his hand to pull Lukas up from the ground. Eye to eye, he squeezed his grandson's hand with affection and headed into the showroom.

Chapter 7

Blain poured Lucy, Sophie and himself a glass of wine and settled the bottle back in the ice bucket.

'This is nice,' Lucy said, 'we haven't done this for ages.'

'Because you've been in love, Luv,' Blain reminded her. 'Sophie and I had to wait for the first throes of love's bloom to fade in order to see you… or something like that.'

Lucy rolled her eyes and Sophie laughed.

'It is good to be here again, the three of us,' Sophie agreed. 'It's been a weird month.'

Blain sipped his wine, put his menu down and studied Sophie. 'For you more than us. I've had a busy month at the salon, but I didn't find out I'm psychic, help the police close two cases, and read three people's tea leaves on Monday.'

Sophie chuckled. 'I don't do tea leaves, but thanks for the vote of support.' She turned to Lucy. 'Is everything alright, you know, with you and Lukas?'

Lucy nodded. 'Why, has he said something? Have you seen something?'

'No, not at all,' Sophie said holding up her hands in a

surrender gesture. 'It's just a girlfriend question because I have no love life of my own, and am living vicariously through you.'

Lucy smiled and relaxed. 'Oh, right. I guess it is like all new relationships, you go through the wildly enamoured stage and then you have to decide if you are compatible. He is a closed book.'

'Is he?' Sophie asked surprised.

'You don't think he is?' Lucy asked, a hint of challenge in her response which Sophie read.

She shrugged. 'I wouldn't have a clue, I was just surprised, probably because Alfred is so open and Orli is so touchy-feely. I thought it might run in the family.'

Lucy appeared satisfied with the answer. She was touchy tonight, Sophie thought and vowed to let Blain ask the love questions for the rest of the night.

Lucy explained: 'Well, to be honest, I thought once we got to know each other more he'd be more affectionate, or reveal himself more, but he doesn't show me any emotional depth.'

'He's a guy,' Blain said with a grunt. 'You're expecting too much.'

'Maybe,' she agreed. 'But I do have news...'

They both looked at her expectantly, stopping only long enough to thank the waiter as their meals arrived.

'Well given what you just said about Lukas, I'm guessing you're not engaged. Pregnant?' Blain asked.

Lucy grimaced. 'Good grief, no, I've got a huge modelling contract coming up in two months.'

'Ah that was my guess, that you got a new modelling job,' Sophie said and looked excited for her.

Lucy laughed. 'I have, but that's not my news.' She leaned forward and lowered her voice. 'My ex is back in town and he wants to see me.'

'Ooh, this can't be good, or is it good?' Blain asked confused.

'The Swedish vet?' Sophie asked.

'Yes, and he misses me and wants to talk about reconciling,' she said.

Sophie's lips thinned with worry. What would this do to Lukas, and more importantly, could his reaction hurt her friend?

'How do you feel about it? You two were always so full-on, and one week on, the next week off,' Sophie said.

'I know,' Lucy agreed. 'But I've never had a passionate relationship or felt for anyone so deeply as I feel for Anders. I'm just not sure I can take the emotional ride again.'

Blain nodded. 'I get that. You've recovered, got used to being without them, and then they swan back in and turn everything on its head.'

'Exactly,' Lucy said appreciating her seafood salad and Blain's analysis. 'You can't tell Lukas though,' she looked at Sophie with alarm.

'Of course not,' Sophie said.

Lucy continued. 'I don't have to decide right now, but if I do, it will be a choice between passion and the rollercoaster ride, versus stable and closed book.'

'I know what I'd pick,' Blain said before Sophie commented. 'I'd go the passion, even if you fight like crazy. You'll be bored with stable down the track and always wonder if you did the right thing.'

Lucy nodded. 'That's kind of where I am heading too, but I did make myself sick with Anders, being on and off is wearing on the heart.' She rubbed her hand over her heart as if assuring it all would be well. 'And you, Soph? What would you choose?'

Sophie thought for a moment and knew she had to be diplomatic. 'I don't think it's a choice between passion and stability. Lukas is a really good-looking guy and a bit mysterious. He's a fair-haired dark horse!'

'He likes you, a lot,' Lucy said as if it was Sophie's fault, and then Sophie realised where the tension was coming from.

'Not like that though,' she assured Lucy. 'He met me first. If he was interested in me, he'd be going out with me.'

'Would you go out with him?'

For the love of God, Sophie thought, this is going nowhere good.

Sophie shrugged. 'I think Murdoch is interesting...' she glanced to Blain who picked up her vibe.

'Ooh, how is the handsome detective?'

'Still handsome, and grumpy but I think that's his partner rubbing off on him.'

The subject drifted elsewhere but Sophie could sense the mild animosity coming from Lucy. Was Lukas at risk of losing his relationship because of her, she wondered. Would she go out with Lukas? Then she remembered it didn't matter, she had seen Lukas and Lucy marrying when she first had her visions. Unless the future can change, Sophie already knew which way Lucy's heart was going to go. What she didn't know was how that would play out for her relationship with Lucy and Lukas.

Chapter 8

'So, should I stay with him or leave?' the woman sitting opposite Sophie asked, folding her hands in her lap and looking as if she would do whatever Sophie instructed.

Sophie took a deep breath. She was getting more confident at reading and less frazzled if she could not immediately respond. Her own research conducted by visiting other clairvoyants had helped Sophie find her own style, and Miss Sharpe's encouragement and feedback had also given her confidence.

Miss Sharpe had shown in Penelope Burton, a first-time client, and now the two women sat poised for the reading. They were seated at a small round table with a white lace tablecloth, far enough away from the window not to be seen by outsiders, but with plenty of light filling the room. Miss Sharpe had made them both a cup of tea and while Penelope sipped hers, Sophie opened Daphne's – now her own – glasses case and slipped on the glasses. With a bit of ceremony and trying to get focussed, Sophie placed her palms flat on the table. She made eye contact with the 40-

plus, expensively groomed client, who Sophie was sure had regularly had Botox, amongst other beauty treatments. Penelope's expressions seemed limited.

'You would like to know whether or not to leave your husband?' Sophie asked and frowned.

Penelope nodded. 'Well, it's a little more complex than that. I met him when I was very young and he was a singer in a rock band – I was 18, he was 45. He was quite a star in our London circle, so bad and sexy,' she said and smiled at the memory. 'We moved to Australia two decades ago and now he just enjoys gardening and reading. He's nearly eighty and I'm going on 53. I'm at my sexual peak! Should I stay or is he going to die soon and I'd be better to wait?'

Sophie restrained a laugh of surprise. 'Well, that's certainly a question that I haven't been asked before,' she said and then she felt a wave of sadness. 'You've been together 35 years, it must be love.'

'We're very different people these days,' Penelope said and Sophie nodded her understanding. It wasn't for her to sit in judgement, Great Aunt Daphne would be the first to remind her of that.

Sophie looked at the images appearing around Penelope's head concerning the future and the question asked. She could feel Penelope scrutinising her and waiting for an answer.

'Without seeing your husband, I can't tell you what his future is or how long his lifeline is,' she said. That wasn't quite true because Sophie could see images of Penelope at her husband's funeral. She continued: 'But I can tell you that there is more happiness to come for the pair of you.'

'Really?' Penelope asked surprised. 'He doesn't like to go anywhere, and he's not interested in catching up with most of my friends. We used to have so much fun. We love live bands and dancing... I miss him.'

Sophie nodded. 'It appears there is some fun coming your way. There's an awards ceremony – a music one by the looks of it and he is getting an award. Lots of people there, all on their feet clapping, and you are with him.'

'Oh, how exciting,' she gushed.

'It looks like a hall of fame award,' Sophie continued, 'but might be best not to tell him that and let him enjoy the surprise.'

'I will. What else can you see?' Penelope asked.

'I can see a magazine spread... photos being taken of you and him around your house.'

'I'm renovating, perhaps they do a story on us at home! Is it *Vogue Living*?'

'I can't tell that, sorry,' Sophie said, again trying not to laugh. 'But you both look very stylish and I imagine he will attract some fangirls after that.' Sophie added the last bit for effect. She knew if the marriage were to end, she could do nothing to save it, but it didn't hurt for her to do a little counselling she figured. 'Oh... and goodness!'

'What?' Penelope leaned forward eagerly.

'Does your husband play the drums?'

'He does, why, what is he doing?'

'Well, it looks like a gig with a few other oldies, all playing and enjoying themselves. I think you are going to be busy.'

Penelope clapped her hands with excitement. They spoke a while longer and then Miss Sharpe appeared and took Penelope away to organise payment which included a generous tip, Penelope's praise ringing in Sophie's ears.

Penelope's husband only had four years of life left, and they would be big years. Sophie saw he would spend it happily married, never knowing that his lifetime bride had planned to leave.

*****

Miss Sharpe returned and smiled on seeing Sophie's expression.

'Good grief,' Sophie said, and Miss Sharpe chuckled. 'Thank goodness she came and saw me, I would have hated for that marriage to end when... well, let's just say life is short.'

'Well done you,' Miss Sharpe said. 'She was most excited when she left. I believe Lukas is about to arrive.'

Sophie bristled and turned immediately to the driveway. There was no car in sight.

'Don't be fearful,' Miss Sharpe said.

'I'm not frightened of him, just angry. Okay, maybe after seeing his yellow eyes I'm a little freaked out,' Sophie said.

'He would never hurt you, ever.'

'I wish I could be as sure of that. Yesterday, I thought I'd be cut to ribbons by flying shards of glass.' She shuddered at the memory and turned as the sound of a car on the gravel caught her attention and Lukas pulled up into the parking lot in his black Lexus sedan. It suited him, Sophie thought as she studied the tall, handsome man as he alighted from his car. She saw him take a deep breath and exhale, and

Sophie softened, feeling relief that he too was as anxious as she was, maybe more.

Sophie turned back around but Miss Sharpe had gone. She quickly put away her glasses in their case and consulted a mirror to ensure she was in order. Turning on hearing their voices, her eyes locked with Lukas and they both looked sheepish.

'I suspect Sophie cannot drink any more tea but would you care for one?'

'No but thank you, Miss Sharpe,' Lukas said, glancing at her and then returning his attention to Sophie.

'I shall leave you both to speak,' Miss Sharpe said and disappeared to her office area.

They stared at each other momentarily and then spoke at the same time.

'I've come—'

'Would you like to—'

They stopped and smiled.

'Please, take a seat,' Sophie said and indicated the two large chairs near the window. Lukas nodded and followed her there.

Lukas cleared his throat, shuffled, looked uncomfortable and then settled on leaning forward with his elbows on his knees and his hands clasped.

'Please accept my apology for my actions yesterday and for frightening you,' he said. 'It wasn't my intention, not for a moment.'

Sophie nodded her thanks, accepting his apology. Holding his gaze, she said: 'I am sorry for pushing you and baiting you, causing you to get so angry. That was not my intention.'

'You're good at it,' he added, and smiled before she snapped back.

Sophie narrowed her eyes at him. 'You're as stubborn as a mule.'

'Know many mules?' Lukas asked.

'No, but if I did, I'd call it Lukas.'

'That so?' he asked smiling. 'Well, every time I come across a roadblock, I now think of you.'

'I guess there are worse things I could bring to mind.'

They stopped sparring for a moment and regarded each other with amusement.

Lukas inhaled and sat back. 'Grandfather and Orli do not think we will be able to work together, that I can protect you given our... clashes.'

Sophie's eyes widened in surprise and she looked away while she gathered her thoughts. She never thought this would be an outcome of their sparring, and she didn't want to be 'unpartnered' from him. Sophie felt slightly pained by the thought, having come to think of him as her new protector through all this change.

She noted he waited patiently for her to speak and wondered if he was trying to read her mind. Sophie was glad he struggled with it; she didn't want him to understand the thoughts racing through hers at this time.

'What do you think?' she asked. 'Do you want to stay as my protector?'

'I'd like to know first, your thoughts.' She went to protest but Lukas held up his hands. 'It is just that you don't seem to have a great deal of faith in my processes. Grandfather and Orli are both spiritually stronger than me,' he said. 'You may be better paired, even safer, with one of them. Maybe Orli, because Grandpa is not a young man.'

Sophie wished she could put the glasses on and understand what Lukas wanted, what their future would be.

'I am sorry if I have pushed you and made you feel that way,' Sophie said in all honesty. 'It's not a reflection on you, but sadly a reflection on me.' She gave a small shrug. 'I've always pushed and fought for what I've wanted. I think being an only child, I've rarely not got my way. Being told no, and negotiating, is not one of my skills.'

Lukas smiled. 'I'm not dissimilar. That's probably why we clash. We are both right and want our own processes to win out.'

'I want to work together,' Sophie said going out on a limb and then she said in a rush of words: 'I want you to be my protector. I promise I'll try harder. But…' she added quickly, 'only if that is what you want. If you want out, I will understand, of course, no drama.' She stopped speaking.

Lukas breathed out, relieved. 'I want to stay a team too. I want to protect you. I'm sure once we get our rhythm going, we'll be formidable, like Daphne and Grandpa.'

Sophie smiled and extended her hand and they shook, a spark making both of them jump back.

'Ow, you gave me a shock,' Sophie said wide-eyed.

'I thought you gave it to me,' Lukas said.

'It probably came from the same place that your power came from that destroyed the crystal yesterday!'

'I assure you, if I gave you an electric shock from that power supply, you would be across the room!'

They smiled at each other, Sophie shaking her head.

'Miss Sharpe will already know,' Sophie said, 'should we tell Alfred?'

Lukas tapped his temple. 'He knows. I felt him a moment ago reading me, he's very good at it.'

They turned to see Miss Sharpe entering, a smile on her face at their decision. 'Detective Murdoch Ashcroft is arriving,' she said, and again moments later his car appeared.

Lukas stood, wary and Sophie also got to her feet.

'The raven,' Lukas said under his breath, his eyes narrowing.

'Shall I send him away or show him through,' Miss Sharpe asked.

Sophie glanced at Lukas.

'It will be okay, won't it? You meeting him?' she asked. 'He doesn't know.'

'No, I don't think he knows,' Lukas said. 'I need to get going anyway. Introduce us as you might normally and I'll be quick to leave.'

'Thank you, Miss Sharpe,' Sophie said as Miss Sharpe headed out to greet Murdoch.

Sophie turned to Lukas.

'Will he sense it?' she asked.

'I doubt it, not if he is not open to it,' Lukas responded.

'What's our story, should he ask?'

Sophie bit her lip, thinking on her feet. 'You've come about my new glasses.'

'Excellent,' Lukas said.

'You're comfortable with a white lie?' Sophie studied him.

'If I wasn't, myself and everyone I love would be dead years ago at the hands of witch hunters,' he said with a shrug.

'Trust me, they are still around. Call it self-preservation.'

'Well, when you put it like that,' Sophie said in agreement.

They heard the footfalls of Miss Sharpe and Murdoch in the hallway and turned as they entered.

'Detective,' Sophie said.

'Sorry, am I interrupting?' he asked, stopping just inside the doorway and studying Lukas.

'No, I'm just leaving,' Lukas said, moving towards the doorway where Murdoch stood.

'Detective Ashcroft, this is an old family friend, Lukas Lens. His family own the *Optical Illusion* store,' Sophie said and watched as the men shook hands. They were the same height, but Murdoch was wider in the shoulders. Their colouring contrasting, as was the tradition of the Harley and Hadley lines.

'Ah, yes, Sophie has mentioned you before,' Murdoch said.

Lukas nodded and gave him a half-hearted smile, trying to read Murdoch's thoughts. He turned to Sophie. 'Thank you, I'll catch up with you soon.'

'Of course,' she said, and turning to show Murdoch to a chair, she saw outside the birds... the doves and ravens landing around her window, and on the two men's cars.

Chapter 9

Through the large arched windows, Murdoch was watching Lukas like he was a criminal in the making, until he realised Sophie was studying him. He cleared his throat and turned his attention to her.

'Sorry to interrupt your date,' he said, fishing.

'Hardly. Lukas is going out with Lucy... you know my friend, Lucy? He's here about my new glasses, a house call of sorts,' Sophie said, sticking to the story they agreed upon. She quite liked the idea, so the embellishment was achievable.

'Right. So, how's your day going?' he asked, taking a seat opposite Sophie and trying but failing not to glance outside once again. 'What's with the birds? You and your Aunt Daphne... are you bird channelers?'

Sophie grinned. 'Yes, you've got it in one. When I'm not acting, solving crimes, or reading people's futures, I'm out in the yard practising my bird calls. I'm particularly good at the yellow-breasted wood-warbler.'

Murdoch put his head back and laughed at the absurdity of it.

'Is there such a bird?'

'Bound to be,' she said, grinning.

On seeing Lukas's car leave the gates, he returned his attention to her. She looked beautiful; he didn't like to admit it because he didn't want to fall for her. He wanted a professional relationship like he had with Daphne, and to not be compromised in his feelings when he came to ask for her help. Love made him weak, he was still recovering from the disaster that was his last relationship.

'So, what do I owe the pleasure, Muddy,' she teased him. 'Nice suit by the way,' she said, admiring his dark grey suit, crisp white shirt and blue tie.

'This old thing,' Murdoch said and made her laugh. 'I am sorry to interrupt your busy day of house and bird calls...'

'I've done one reading and had two visitors. I haven't really started yet. And you? Don't tell me you've got another case already?' She frowned.

'No, you can relax, I'm not here to put you to work,' Murdoch said, with a smile. 'Well actually I am, but there's no deadline... consider it a proposition.'

'Ooh, that sounds interesting.' She sat back and folded her legs which he found distracting.

'It's about Gerard.'

Sophie looked disappointed. 'Your grumpy partner, hmm, not so interesting.'

Murdoch relaxed. 'He retires next year, and he's got a cold case that weighs heavily on him. He often says it's the one that haunts him. I was hoping you might bring him some peace.'

'Are his legs broken? He can't come here and ask me?'

'They're both broken,' Murdoch confirmed, and she scoffed at him. 'You've got to cut him some slack. He's a grumpy old bastard, who doesn't want to believe in anything he can't see, but he grudgingly has to acknowledge you and Daphne have helped us.'

'Good of him. Does he know you are talking to me about it?'

'Absolutely. He's open to working with you. But he thought I might like the opportunity to catch up with you and brief you... you know, us "young people hanging out" and all that,' he said, imitating Gerard.

Sophie grinned. 'You do Gerard very well. Okay, tell me about the case. If it's as boring as Gerard, I can't promise I'll do it.'

'C'mon his mother loves him.'

Sophie smirked.

'Okay. Thirty years ago, a beauty queen, Cassie Delaney, went missing at her 21st birthday party and was found dead...'

Sophie held up her hand. 'You had me at beauty queen. Tell Grumpy I'm in. But I have one condition.'

'Do tell?' Murdoch said.

'It is unconditional,' she said again, making her point.

'Yeah, I hear you. What is it?'

'He has to work with me, and me alone on the case.'

Murdoch chuckled then sobered seeing she was serious.

Sophie continued. 'Gerard can't send you as his envoy or send me notes. I'm not saying I don't enjoy my quality time with you,' she said with a smirk, 'but it's him and me on the case.'

Murdoch frowned. 'Why would you put both of you through that?'

Sophie shrugged. 'I like a challenge and he needs a shake-up. When he retires, I want him to mention me at his retirement party farewell.'

Murdoch laughed. 'Yeah, good luck with that.'

'Want to put a bet on it,' she said extending her hand.

'You're on. Money or reward?' Murdoch asked, rising to shake her hand and preparing to depart.

'The loser takes the winner to the restaurant of their choice, no expense spared,' Sophie said and rose too. They shook on the bet. 'That way I get to enjoy seeing you suffer as well.'

Murdoch gave her a wry look. 'Start saving, I've got a place in mind and it's not cheap.'

Chapter 10

Sophie quickly sent Lucy a message to see if she was okay and if there had been any advancement on her ex-boyfriend, Anders, being back in town. Within minutes Lucy replied they were catching up tonight to talk. Sophie was grateful she hadn't known that detail when she met with Lukas, in case he could read her. Alfred said he was improving in that skill.

A knock on her office door interrupted her thoughts and a girl about her own age bounded in. She was shorter and wider than Sophie, with brown skin, dark hair featuring a pink streak in the fringe, and wearing bright flower-printed, fitted pants and top. She had a radiant smile.

'Hi!'

Sophie rose. 'Hello, sorry, I didn't know I had another reading. Miss Sharpe has gone to the bank. But that's no problem—'

The young woman laughed cutting her off. 'Ooh, I'd love a reading, but no, I'm not booked in. I'm Melino, call me Mel.'

Sophie still looked confused but accepted Mel's hand and shook it. She felt very dull in her navy dress and tan shoes when Mel was so colourful.

'I work in the *Sport for Every Girl* office... one of the community groups here... back of the building,' she said waiting for Sophie to catch up.

'Oh my God, I'm an idiot,' Sophie said, 'of course. I've seen you around. I'm Sophie.'

'I know you are. That was amazing what you did saving that kid from the nappers,' Mel shook her head in disbelief.

'That was lucky,' Sophie said and briefly told the story again about how the nephew nearly left. 'So, *Sport for Every Girl*, huh?' she said and studied Mel. 'I thought every community group in the building was a pet project of Aunt Daphne's. I didn't know she was into sport.'

'Surprised us too when we got the call offering us the discounted office space,' Mel said, planting herself on the edge of the table and folding her arms across her chest.

Sophie liked how instantly comfortable they were with each other.

Mel continued. 'Your aunt sponsored about half a dozen young girls through World Vision.'

'She did?' Sophie interrupted, surprised.

'She did!' Mel laughed. 'One of them won a netball scholarship to Australia and then your aunt just kept following her. The community group I work for had her as an ambassador, so your aunt sponsored us. Ta-dah!'

'There you go,' Sophie said.

'That's it,' Mel agreed. 'Anyway, just thought I'd drop in and introduce myself. I saw the birds earlier... the ravens and the doves. Odd, huh?'

'Yeah, Aunt Daphne used to attract them as well,' Sophie said with a glance outside. The birds were gone, thank goodness. She didn't elaborate.

Mel nodded. 'My great grandmother had the gift, second sight, the curse, whatever you want to call it. She practised Tongan medicine – people would come from all over the island to be healed by her.'

Sophie returned her gaze to Mel with interest.

'Do you have it, the gift?' Sophie asked.

'Sometimes. I don't do what you do, but I sense things and I work with potions.'

'Like herbal remedies and cures?' Sophie asked.

'Exactly. I believe everything we need is in nature, and just add a dollop of magic,' she said and grinned.

Sophie laughed. 'I agree.'

Miss Sharpe's car came up the driveway and was driven into its designated spot.

'I should get going,' Mel sobered, her eyes alight with curiosity. 'I just dropped in because the last time I saw that happen – the birds gathering as they did before – there were witches in the house! So exciting.'

*****

Miss Sharpe greeted Mel as they passed in the hallway. She entered the office to find Sophie standing by the bay window.

'Ah, you've met Mel. She's got the witching in her that young lady, she's special,' Miss Sharpe said.

'She mentioned she makes potions,' Sophie said and sat on the window ledge. 'Speaking of witching, you know what tomorrow is, don't you?'

Miss Sharpe smiled and nodded. She turned to fuss with a vase of flowers… one bloom had dared to fall out of alignment.

'It has been a huge month, Sophie. But you don't have to make your decision tomorrow, even though we said take a month and see how you feel about the role.' Miss Sharpe moved to adjust the curtains to reduce the glare. 'If you need longer, there is no hurry.'

'Thank you, Miss Sharpe. But actually, I have made up my mind,' Sophie said running her hands down the length of her skirt, one of her fidgeting gestures. 'I can't believe all that has happened in a month.'

Miss Sharpe lowered herself momentarily onto the chair opposite the bay window. She never leaned back or sat as if she intended to stay. Sophie came over to join her.

'I never thought we would get this far, I must confess,' Miss Sharpe said, clasping her hands in her lap. 'But I am thrilled by our working relationship, and for fear of sounding patronising, I am so proud of who you are and what you have become, my dear Sophie. But don't let that sway you. You will always have my respect.'

Sophie found herself uncharacteristically emotional. Perhaps because for the first time in her life she felt she had earned the praise; it had been generous and the giver's opinion was important to her.

'I would not, and could not do it without you, Miss Sharpe. Aunt Daphne is right… was right… you are the backbone of our team.'

Miss Sharpe nodded her head with thanks.

Sophie continued. 'It became very clear to me at my last audition what I wanted to do; I don't need an extension or even to wait until tomorrow.' She took a deep breath and announced: 'I wish to take on this role full time. I want to carry on Aunt Daphne's work, see her clients and my new clients, help the police, work with you, Miss Sharpe. If I stay, will you stay?'

Miss Sharpe clapped her hands together with delight. 'Absolutely.'

'Aunt Daphne was right,' Sophie said, 'I am going to be a clairvoyant. I can't believe all the years she told me that and I used to get so furious at her.' Sophie laughed.

'She said a lot more than that,' Miss Sharpe reminded Sophie, 'and I believe she was right when she said "You will be one of the greatest clairvoyants of your time".'

Chapter 11

Lukas braced himself. His grandfather stood further away from him, as they faced each other in a copse of trees in the Botanic Gardens, away from the public eye. Back in the *Optical Illusion* store, Orli kept the business running. The two men needed somewhere where they could practice harnessing anger and energy without destroying the surroundings, in particular the glass, around them. Alfred had placed a charm around the area from tree to tree so no person, animal or plant could be harmed.

'You are still hesitant to spar with me, Lukas,' his grandfather said with mild frustration.

Lukas rolled his eyes. 'Stop reading me.'

'It's not that I seek out your mind to do so, I promise you. Normally I would have to concentrate to read you, but sometimes your thoughts are so loud they push into mine and distract me,' Alfred assured him. 'Like now.'

'You can't blame me. I don't want to hurt you, Grandpa,' Lukas said.

'Nor do I want to hurt you, but there's more chance of that than the other way around, I assure you.'

He studied his handsome young grandson and with that said, Alfred flipped Lukas to the ground without moving a muscle.

'Christ,' Lukas muttered hitting the ground hard enough that he was almost winded. He went to rise and Alfred did it again.

'I hate it when you do that. You could have warned me,' he said.

'I need you to be angry so that you will lash out. Otherwise, I can't teach you how to harness that anger,' Alfred said. 'Stop thinking, Lukas, empty your mind.'

Lukas tried not to think about anything in particular and pushed himself to his feet.

'Now, you will attempt to knock me backwards with your power,' Alfred said.

Lukas raised his hand to do so, but could not do it. His eyes remained pale blue, his energy neutral.

Alfred sighed. 'Forgive me, lad,' he said and in four quick moves, without himself moving an inch, he thrust Lukas back against the tree, then to the ground, and as Lukas scrambled up, he knocked him down again and back to where he started.

Lukas's jaw locked in pain and anger and his eyes flared yellow. It wasn't enough yet and Alfred knew it. He repeated the four steps again, hearing Lukas swear in anger and pain.

And then he had him. In anger or self-defence, Lukas aimed his yellow stare at his grandfather and sent a surge of power. Alfred's hand went straight up and stopped it midway between them.

'Send it to the tree, Lukas,' he ordered his grandson while holding the orb of power between them. 'Call it back and send it to your right.'

The ball of energy waned as Lukas could see the shape of his grandfather again and the power dispersed.

Alfred sighed. 'Okay, this calls for drastic action.'

Lukas braced and Alfred chuckled. 'Relax for a moment, I'm not going to throw you again.'

'That old trick, disarm the opponent,' Lukas said narrowing his eyes with suspicion.

And then right in front of his eyes, Alfred did something Lukas did not know his grandfather was capable of doing. He changed.

*****

Sophie finished her last reading for the day. She never did more than three in a day, although with the booking requests she received, she could read all day if she needed the cash. She bid Miss Sharpe goodbye for the afternoon – Miss Sharpe was enjoying her part-time hours – and making herself a cup of tea, Sophie determined to spend the next hour doing some research on Cassie Delaney, the beauty queen.

'Thirty years ago,' Sophie muttered, 'Gerard must have been a young gun.' She smiled at the thought and wondered if he was grumpy then too. She put Cassie's name in the search engine and sat back.

'Wow, still lots of interest in Cassie, obviously.'

Sophie opened a story about the 30th anniversary of the beauty queen's murder and studied the photos.

'Oh, Cassie, you were gorgeous.' Sophie noted Cassie looked young for her 21 years. Her small heart-shaped face, large eyes, and long dark hair made her look sweet and innocent.

'What happened to you, Cassie?'

Sophie clicked on each online story, at first reading the headlines then scanning each one for a different angle or something new:

The killing of the 21-year-old beauty queen and trainee teacher remains one of the most sensational mysteries in the country.

'...it has been 30 years since 21-year-old Cassandra Delaney was found murdered in her car and her killer is still at large.'

She opened another headline:

'After an extensive search, police found Cassie Delaney's body in her car at the bottom of the creek near her home, one week after her disappearance.'

And another story:

'Cassandra was not a drug user, not known to use any substances, but had overdosed and died before coming to rest at the bottom of the creek.'

Sophie gasped, her mind racing. Good grief, who was she with when taking the drugs? Did she drive into the creek on a high? How did she get there? Was the killer a guest at her 21st birthday party? She read on:

'Police interviewed more than 80 people with no witnesses coming forward.

'Cassie's best friends are distraught and frightened.

'No charges laid in Cassandra Delaney murder.

'The father of murdered beauty queen, Cassandra Delaney, was found dead today of a drug overdose. Rumours of his involvement in his daughter's death plagued the family. Parallels are now being drawn between Mr Delaney's death and that of his daughter.

'Cassie Delaney's mother tells of her agony; the pain that never leaves as the 30th anniversary of Cassie's murder looms.'

Sophie clicked on another page and a large photo of Cassie Delaney filled the screen. She was smiling coyly as if she was shy with the person taking the photo. Sophie zoomed in to look into Cassie's eyes.

'We'll find who did this to you, Cassie,' she said, to the woman who at 21 at the time of her death, was seven years younger than Sophie today. If Cassie was alive now, she would be in her fifties, maybe with her own family. 'I promise, I'll do my best.'

Chapter 12

Standing across from Lukas was the man who might be his enemy, the man from Hadley's line of descendants and the current raven – Murdoch Ashcroft.

Lukas started, shocked.

Alfred could read his grandson's mind – it was scrambling with what he was facing. But he didn't give his grandson time to process the change, to realise he wasn't really in danger. Alfred hit him with the same force, one time, two times, three times, until Lukas fought back.

With the speed of light, Alfred stopped Lukas's enraged ball of power hovering it between them again.

'Harness it,' he ordered Lukas and was delighted when Lukas pushed it harder towards Alfred. He laughed with pleasure at his fightback.

Seeing the raven laugh enraged Lukas and he pushed harder, his strength impressive but no match for Alfred's.

'Capture and divert it, Lukas,' Alfred order, the words coming from Murdoch's mouth. 'Do it!' he ordered penetrating Lukas's mind with the order as well.

Lukas's eyes narrowed, and he focussed on the ball of fire between them, the surging power force, and with his jaw locked and his yellow eyes maintaining the rage, he moved the power force slowly away from Alfred and towards the tree. With a quick nod, he sent it hurtling towards a huge Lilly Pilly tree. The ball hit Alfred's protective field before it reached the tree and burst into flames, disappearing.

When Lukas turned back, the figure of Murdoch Ashcroft was gone and Alfred stood there.

'Well done! That's how it is done, lad,' Alfred said and Lukas exhaled.

'You freaked me out, Grandpa. I didn't know you could do that, why didn't I know that?' he asked.

'I've never needed to do it in front of you, I guess.'

'Can I do that?' Lukas asked.

'I don't know. Can you? You can be in two places at once, so in time, perhaps you will change form. Now that you are protecting Sophie, you have a lot to learn about your own capabilities. Orli and I can help you.'

'Witch boot camp?' Lukas said with a grin and started walking towards his grandfather and Alfred stopped him.

'We're not done yet.'

Lukas stopped. 'You want me to do it again a few more times?'

'No. Instead of defending yourself from my fireball, I want you to defend me.'

Lukas looked worried and Alfred held up his hand.

'Clear your mind,' Alfred said. 'I am going to be attacked. You are going to be angry about it, but then you'll realise there is no danger and you can't hurt the attacker. So, you will call back your anger and destroy the source. Do you understand?'

Lukas nodded. 'As I should have done in the shop the other day with Sophie when my anger put us all at risk.'

'In a manner of speaking.'

And then Alfred was on fire.

'Christ!' Lukas yelled and saw a fire demon standing in front of his grandfather. His eyes flared yellow, the power surge to destroy the fire demon came in a rush that he did not think he was capable of, and then the demon changed to Sophie.

Lukas gasped in surprise and struggled to pull back his power. It was taking too long, which made him angrier and the power stronger, hotter, more dangerous.

With a flick of his hand, Alfred destroyed Lukas's power surge, dissolved the demon and returned to his form, as Lukas staggered backward, spent.

'Okay, we are not going to conquer everything on your first day,' Alfred said.

Lukas shook his head. 'If that wasn't a trial, I would have burnt Sophie to death. Can we go again?'

'Of course, if you're up to it. We can go as many times as you want, lad.'

Lukas nodded and Alfred braced. This time, Alfred chose a different enemy – a demonic figure who appeared to be enraged and about to harm Alfred.

Lukas reacted hard and fast to the image and hurtled a flame at the demon, and then Alfred changed to Orli. Lukas gasped and grabbed at his power, pulling it back towards him. He cast the power to the side and watched it evaporate.

Orli disappeared and Alfred stood there, whole again. Alfred grinned and gave him a round of applause. 'Much better this time.'

Lukas turned to his grandfather, gave him a weak smile, and leaned over, placing his hands on his knees and pulling in several long breaths. 'You scared the hell out of me.'

'Then we won't repeat the exercise today. Besides, the element of surprise has gone.'

'You're right, and I've had enough, thanks,' Lukas said rising. 'Your skills are amazing.'

'So will yours be, my boy, by the time we're finished with you,' Alfred said. 'But expect the unexpected. The best way to test you is for you not to be prepared.'

Lukas gave a small groan and a nod. 'I'll sleep with one eye open.'

Alfred laughed and affectionately patted his grandson's shoulder. The two men headed back to *Optical Illusion*. Alfred turned back and with a flick of his wrist, removed the protection order.

*****

Sophie loved the sanctuary of her apartment. She entered, put the chain on the door, and slipping off her shoes, sat for a few moments to talk with Bette Davis and stroke the fluffy white cat's soft fur. After they had shared the events of the day, Sophie rose, grabbed her shoes and bag, and headed to her bedroom, changing into leisurewear.

A sharp rap brought her back to the door.

'It's me,' Lucy's voice said from the other side and Sophie slipped the chain across, pulling her friend in with a hug.

'Sorry to come unannounced,' Lucy said, looking beautiful even in casual wear – jeans, a pale pink pullover and white sandshoes.

'Don't be crazy, it's great to see you,' Sophie said and locked the door behind Lucy. 'What will you have, wine, coffee or tea?'

'Better make it wine,' Lucy said.

'Uh oh,' Sophie said. 'Make yourself at home.' She studied her friend momentarily before making her way to the kitchen, grabbing two glasses and a bottle of white wine. As an afterthought, she grabbed the packet of corn chips from the cupboard... Miss Sharpe never allowed her to miss lunch but that seemed like hours ago and she needed to stay sober in case the discussion got heavy.

Sophie could hear Lucy murmuring to Bette Davis and she silently prayed Lucy hadn't called it off with Lukas. That would be awkward now that her future was attached to his for as long as she did what she did... and that was going to be a long while yet.

She entered the lounge room and Lucy rose to help her.

'You pour the wine, I'll close the curtains and light some scented candles,' Sophie said, in an attempt to create a relaxing atmosphere.

'How was your day?' Lucy asked stalling, as she half-filled two wine glasses.

'Just the usual,' Sophie joked as she lit two candles and inhaled the jasmine scent. 'I read a few fortunes, met a witch or two, told Miss Sharpe I was going to stay in the business full-time.' She blew out the match.

'What? Really! That's great!' Lucy exclaimed.

'Congratulations on making a decision, either way. But I suspected you were going that way,' she said with a knowing look.

'I must admit I still had some doubts until I went to that last audition. Then, it was really weird, I just didn't want to be there. It suddenly was very clear.' Sophie settled beside Bette Davis and accepted the glass of wine. They clinked glasses, toasted their health and sipped. 'It was the weirdest thing,' Sophie continued facing Lucy on the dimpled couch opposite her. 'I don't have the ambition for it anymore and I never thought I would say that. I'm tired of auditions, and even though I love the accolades, the need is not burning inside me.'

Lucy smiled. 'Well, that's great. I wish I could see so clearly. I'm so exhausted from thinking all the time.'

'I understand that completely,' Sophie said. 'Are you okay?'

'Yes. No,' Lucy shook her head and blinked away tears. 'It's my ex, Anders. And Lukas. It's both of them.' She stopped talking and swallowed.

Sophie studied her friend and tried to sum up how she was feeling: 'You still love Anders? He wants you back, but you love Lukas too?'

Lucy nodded, emotion all over her face. 'I don't want to risk losing Lukas, but I've loved Anders for so long that I've always dreamed of being together, and I have some doubts about Lukas.'

'You nearly married Anders once so I know you wanted that,' Sophie said. 'Do you have to make a decision now?'

'I can't string them both along and I can't emotionally deal with it,' Lucy said with alarm in her voice.

'No, of course not. But what if you went away for a few days, or on a model shoot for a week or two? Would it help you with perspective... maybe see who you missed more, who tugs at your heart?'

'I've tried to envision all that,' Lucy said. 'I've tried to imagine life without both of them to see what pained me more.'

'And?' Sophie asked.

'I think it's Anders. He's back, he can legally stay and work here now, and I don't think I can give him up.' Lucy put her glass down and leaned forward. 'You have to tell me, Sophie,' she said. 'This is a decision that could make or break my future, my lifelong happiness. Please tell me which way to choose.'

Sophie put her wineglass down beside Lucy's on the coffee table in front of them.

'I can't Lucy,' she said, horrified at the thought. 'I'm sorry.'

'I'm not asking you to tell me if they'll die before me. Just put the glasses on and tell me which one I should pick now.'

Sophie shook her head. 'I can't because what I see will be the choice you make, but that doesn't mean it is the right one. It's the choice you make. Do you understand?'

'No.' Lucy's lips thinned; her brow furrowed.

'I don't see what is best for you, I just see your future,' Sophie said, trying to explain.

'But you can see our future. You can see if we last, if we're going to be happy,' Lucy insisted.

'All I can see is your destiny that you have chosen. By telling you, you will still wonder all night if you made the right decision choosing that person.'

Lucy inhaled. 'But it will help, it will give me clarity.'

Sophie thought for a moment and was interrupted by Lucy again.

'If I was a stranger coming to you for a reading, you would tell me.'

Sophie nodded. 'That's true, but it's different.'

'How?'

'Because if you didn't know me and I read you, you would still have an element of doubt, you would still make your own choice. But because we know my power is accurate, it will influence you.'

Sophie drank a few sips of wine and said nothing, letting her explanation sink in. She had seen Lucy's future that very first time she put on the glasses as a joke, having just inherited them. Lucy and Blain had agreed the glasses were unattractive and made her look studious. Then, to her shock and dismay, she saw their future around them. Lucy was marrying Lukas, she was fairly sure of that memory, but she had only just met Lukas and looked at the image but for a few seconds. Still, she was fairly confident it wasn't Anders by Lucy's side.

'Okay,' Lucy started again. 'Then since you are not telling me what is best for me but just telling me what choice I make, put me out of my indecision and at least tell me that.'

Sophie bit her lower lip as she thought. 'What happens if I tell you and you're miserable in ten years? Will I be to blame? Or what happens if I tell you that you *will* get a divorce and you pick the other man?' She shook her head. 'I can't tell you. I'm so sorry.'

'So am I,' Lucy said, and getting up, she took her bag and turned once more to Sophie. 'I thought you were more compassionate than that. I thought we were close friends, but like the acting, it seems this is going to your head too.'

Sophie gasped as if Lucy had slapped her. Lucy unlocked the door, let herself out, and departed.

Chapter 13

Detective Gerard Oakley pulled up in his red Holden sedan which had seen better days and was pleased to find Sophie waiting for him out the front of the building. She was holding a bouquet and two cake boxes. Sophie came around the passenger side and got in passing the cake boxes to Gerard who placed them on the back seat one at a time.

'It's not as glamorous as the sedan from the carpool,' Gerard said, 'but Murdoch's got it today.'

'It's fine, I'm partial to old things,' Sophie said with a glance at him and Gerard chuckled.

'You'll keep.'

She buckled up and put the flowers at her feet as they headed out of the grounds.

'Are they for me?' he asked, and Sophie laughed.

'Yeah, this is the best date I've ever had,' she gushed, and he chuckled again and shook his head.

'You've got a mouth.'

'The flowers are for Cassie's mum and the cake for her and her sister.'

'Very thoughtful,' Gerard said. 'Nothing like sweetening up the witnesses to talk.'

'Whatever it takes,' Sophie agreed, straightening down her full black and white skirt so it didn't crease.

'You look very nice, Miss,' Gerard teased, and she laughed.

'Thank you, Sir, I aim to be presentable.'

Gerard straightened up as he looked left and right before pulling onto the nearby busy road and once driving along, he explained: 'So we're seeing Cassie's mum first. She's in an aged care home and a bit dotty according to Cassie's sister, but worth a go.'

'Absolutely,' Sophie said. 'Shame she's not in the family home though, there would be more photos and memories of Cassie, but as you said, worth a go. I read in the paper that Cassie's dad took his own life.'

Gerard nodded. 'Ugly business that. He was one of the few without a rock-solid alibi because he supposedly headed to bed around 11pm and that was about the time she went missing.'

Sophie frowned. 'He's got a house full of guests at his daughter's 21st birthday party, and he was only in his forties?'

'Forty-three,' Gerard confirmed with a glance Sophie's way.

'Right. And he packed it in at eleven... bit strange.'

'Yeah, I thought it was odd... well at the time that was my thought, but he was convincing,' Gerard said.

'Was he sick or did he do shift work?'

'None of the above. Just tired he said, not a party guy... the quiet type.' Gerard shrugged. 'Fair enough I suppose. There have been lots of parties I wanted to leave way before 11pm and I was the host.'

They both chuckled. It was easier being with her than he thought. He expected the journey to be uncomfortable, but they relaxed into each other's company.

He indicated and turned into *Silver Leaf Aged Care*.

'Why do they always have such stupid names?' Sophie asked. 'Aunt Daphne's friend was in *Hope Hill*. Hope for what? A quick death maybe.'

'You're right, I'd much rather live somewhere called *God's Waiting Room*,' Gerard ribbed her and she laughed again.

'Can you park in the shade so we don't melt the cake?' she asked.

He shook his head. 'The things I do for you.'

She grinned and grabbed one of the cake boxes from the backseat. Once parked, Sophie handed Gerard the bouquet, and he led the way to the reception to visit Mrs Iris Delaney.

*****

'I think you will have to tell her,' Alfred said to his grandson, Lukas, as they sat working in companionable silence at the *Optical Illusion store* on the crisp winter morning that had presented itself. The store was peaceful, the glass and crystals reflecting small rainbows around the shop, and the light was just perfect for working unaided by the electrical current.

Alfred concentrated on the books, hoping to have them up to date before Orli arrived for her afternoon optometry appointments; Lukas focused on repairing a timepiece that had seen better days, hoping to resurrect it to its former glory.

Lukas was also playing with his grandfather's mind – not speaking but forming a question in his own mind that protruded into Alfred's thoughts. It would seem odd to anyone present to only hear the responses.

'That's true,' Alfred said, 'I too, am not sure she is ready to know. But if you don't tell her, it becomes a bigger focus for her.'

Lukas worked another question in his mind and Alfred stopped work and looked at him.

'I have full confidence in you, Lukas. Please don't doubt yourself, and I know Sophie trusts you too.'

'Did she say something to you or did you read her?' Lukas asked out loud, surprised.

'I heard her both verbally and mentally,' Alfred said and sighed, tired of being accused of reading everyone as if he were a busybody.

Lukas nodded. 'Sorry.'

'It's not always a gift, but rather intrusive, Lukas, one day you might understand,' Alfred said. 'There are days where I'd love to just be in my own head and have clear thoughts. Your thoughts, for example, press on me some days to such a degree that I have to have a break.'

Lukas looked up from his work. 'Is that why you take brief breaks rather than a lunch break? Are you seeking silence away from me?' he asked concerned, scanning his grandfather's countenance.

Alfred shook his head. 'Nothing so dramatic, I promise you, dear boy.'

Lukas breathed a sigh of relief. He sent his grandfather a thought: 'I can always depart for a while and give you some time away from me.'

'I don't wish that,' Alfred answered out loud, 'and distance would make no difference.'

Lukas thought: 'Tell me how it works with my thoughts.'

Alfred nodded, receiving his question. 'I have to concentrate to read people most times. But you and I work so closely together, and you have been stressed of late. That's why your thoughts are tapping on my mind asking to come in,' he said and smiled.

Lukas grinned at his grandpa and answered out loud: 'Sorry about that, I hope they had the good grace to at least bring a cake when they visit.'

Alfred laughed and shook his head. 'Can't say I've ever read anyone and received a slice of tea cake, but I live in hope.'

They worked on for a while in silence.

'I know, thank you, lad,' Alfred said and smiled not looking up from his work after receiving Lukas's rare show of emotion. 'I feel the same.'

Chapter 14

Sophie and Gerard made their way up the hallway of *Silver Leaf Aged Care* to visit Mrs Iris Delaney. It felt homely, Sophie liked that it was not clinical like a hospital. Iris's room was the last on the left at the end of the hallway.

'We look like father and daughter coming to visit granny,' Gerard said, with a glance into each room as he walked along the hallway.

'Or we could be checking the premises out for you, and I'm the dutiful daughter about to sign you in,' she said and smiled at the idea.

Gerard gave her a smirk. 'I'll give you dutiful in a moment,' he joked.

'Wow, you even sound like a dad!'

Sophie slipped her glasses on so that she could be ready from the moment she saw Iris. The new pair that Orli made had clear glass in the frame's bottom, allowing her to walk without feeling unbalanced, unlike Daphne's glasses which enlarged everything.

A rail-thin woman with short white hair stuck her head

out of her bedroom and startled them both. Her photo and name on the door read *Veronica*. 'Don't steal anything,' she said.

'Wouldn't dream of it,' Sophie said. 'Why, are there thieves about Veronica?'

The woman gave a solemn nod and disappeared just as fast.

'On guard then,' Gerard joked.

'She's going to be here a while,' Sophie said, juggling her handbag and cake box.

He looked inquisitively over the top of the bouquet he was carrying.

'I saw at least another two Christmases around her.' Sophie explained.

As they neared the end of the hallway, another elderly woman appeared.

'Is Barry with you?' she asked.

'Not today sorry, love,' Gerard answered, and she clucked her tongue and walked past them with purpose

'Friend of yours?' Gerard asked Sophie.

'No, but Barry is,' Sophie shot back and made him laugh.

They reached Iris's door and it was ajar. Sophie stepped back and took a deep breath.

'Are you okay?' Gerard asked, and she nodded.

'Just bracing myself. Sometimes I feel the victim's last moments,' she said.

'I'm sorry,' he said genuinely.

She nodded her thanks, surprised by his wave of sympathy when she knew him to be sceptical of her skills.

'Ready,' she said and forced a smile.

Gerard knocked lightly on the door and called out, 'Visitors, Mrs Delaney.'

A frail voice invited them in. 'I was expecting you,' she said and smiled. She was a small woman in stature, with dark brown eyes and white hair to her shoulders. She wore a cotton dress with a cardigan and slip-on tanned moccasins.

'Do you remember me, Mrs Delaney?' Gerard asked accepting the offer of a chair opposite.

'Yes, yes, you're my husband's friend,' she said, confused.

Before he had a chance to correct her, a carer arrived with a tea trolley, having spotted Sophie with the cakebox.

'That's so kind, thank you,' Sophie said and showed Mrs Delaney the cake.

'Ooh, I love a good sponge cake,' she said. 'You know the trick is to always sift the flour in.'

'Is that so? I shall remember that, thank you, Mrs Delaney,' Sophie said. She'd never baked a cake in her life.

They sat and once served, made small talk for a short while. Sophie had told Gerard that she needed direct questions about the subject in order to get results.

'Mrs Delaney, you may remember me, I was the detective who was working on Cassie's case.'

Her breath hitched and then she said his name, 'Detective Oakley.'

'Yes,' he said, surprised, and introduced Sophie as a consultant to the police service. He explained they were revisiting all cold cases and hoped to talk with her about Cassie's case. 'You know I want to bring you peace, and me as well before I retire.'

She smiled and patted his hand. Her lucidity surprised

Sophie. If Mrs Delaney had dementia, it was onset and very early stages.

'Can we talk about the case and Cassie for a little while, Mrs Delaney?' Sophie asked.

'I could talk about Cassie all day long,' she said, her smile sad, and her eyes a little misty at the thought.

'What was your last memory of Cassie?' Sophie asked.

Mrs Delaney closed her eyes momentarily and then opened them and looked straight at Sophie. 'It is as clear to me today as if I was still there. We were having the birthday party in the large downstairs rumpus room; they were called that in those days. Cassie was in the doorway, and she turned back when someone on the dance floor we had made in the corner of the room called her name.'

Mrs Delaney smiled and then closed her eyes again picturing the scene. Her eyes opened wide and then she looked to Gerard as if seeking his endorsement of her memories. 'It wasn't late, was it?'

'No, about 11pm,' he said. 'Late for me these days though.'

'And me,' she chuckled.

Sophie brought her back to Cassie. 'Did she leave the party then? She was in the doorway?'

'Yes, that's right. Were you there?' Mrs Delaney asked.

'No, sadly not,' Sophie said, keeping her responses short to not distract too much from the subject at hand.

Mrs Delaney sighed. 'My Cassie was in the doorway, and someone called her name,' she said again. 'I remember like it was in slow motion, like a film. It's funny that.'

'It's a precious memory, that's why,' Gerard agreed.

'Yes, it is,' Mrs Delaney agreed. 'Cassie smiled and waved

as if she was leaving, but it was her party so I knew she wasn't. She had on a beautiful sea-blue coloured dress, like a ballgown to the knees, with a full skirt, and she always reminded me of that actress, Ali MacGraw... do you know her?'

Gerard answered while Sophie focussed on what she was seeing around her. Images of Cassie, the dress as described by Mrs Delaney, Cassie at the door, waving. She saw other couples dancing, a couple kissing, and she saw Mrs Delaney flitting about.

'Of course, a great beauty was Ali MacGraw,' he said.

'So was Steve McQueen, that boyfriend of Ali's,' Mrs Delaney said teasingly. 'Cassie turned and then she walked out. That was it. She walked away and I never saw her again.'

'Did you ever have a feeling for what might have happened to Cassie?' Sophie asked, 'a hunch, a mother's instinct?'

'I wish I could say I did and I've thought about it, every hour of every day. I know Cassie's father would never have hurt her. They were great mates, adored each other they did.' She took a sip of her tea and Sophie did the same, remembering to keep it social and not to distress Mrs Delaney any more than necessary. 'Did you know Cassie?' she asked Sophie again.

'No, I wish I did,' Sophie said.

'What about Kim?' Gerard asked of Cassie's sister before biting into his tea cake.

Mrs Delaney shook her head. 'Kim seemed to go into her shell after that. She left home soon after. It was too much for her. It won't be long,' she said and smiled.

'Until what, Mrs Delaney?' Sophie asked.

'Until we are all together again. Me, my husband, Cassie, I cannot wait.'

Sophie gave Gerard a nod, she had all she needed. They finished their tea and cake and talked of other things. Mrs Delaney told them about her painting class and they admired her paintings placed around the room. Fifteen minutes later they were back in the car.

'Did you steal anything?' Sophie asked and Gerard laughed.

'Not this time,' he joked. 'So, any insights?'

'Only that Mrs Delaney had nothing to do with it. I saw Cassie in the dress, saw her leave... there was someone in front of her on the other side of the door or several people, but I can't see them without looking through their eyes or Cassie's eyes. She told them to wait. I don't know Ali MacGraw the actress, I'll look her up, but Cassie was gorgeous.'

'She was a beauty, and from what I understand, a sweet and kind girl as well,' he sighed. 'Only the good die young.'

'Makes sense,' Sophie said with a glance his way and they both grinned.

'So will Iris Delaney be with them soon, her family?' Gerard asked.

'She'll have a stroke in her sleep, about four months from now. It will be very quick,' Sophie said.

Gerard nodded. 'God bless her. Right, off to visit Cassie's sister?'

'Absolutely. Let's go see what Kim can show me,' Sophie agreed. 'Are you up for more cake?'

'If duty calls,' he said and gave her a dramatic sigh.

'Clearly, I'm not the only actor in the car,' she laughed.

Chapter 15

Lukas Lens unlocked the drawer which held the volumes of history that entwined his and Sophie's family. He moved several books out of the way until he found the volume he wanted. If Sophie felt she was ready for the witching side of her family history, then he would give it to her, but he still believed it was too early.

Taking a break from studying clocks, watches and all means of timepieces for a while, he sat at the table and chair in the store, as his grandfather and Orli ordered optometry products. He set about to read the entry again that Sophie was keen to read. It had been a long time since he first read it and now that he was Sophie's protector, it was best he got up to speed.

The history of the glasses
An entry by Samuel Rayne. Written on this day of 8 October 1582.

(Note to book beholder: translated from the traditional word to modern speak by Alfred Lens, 24 January 1971)

I am not a witch but my wife, Issbelle, is from witching clan, from a long line of witches. I, however, have just had a witch put to death. Her name was Saghani. She treated me when I fell ill while passing through her village. I did not ask her to save me with witchcraft as I have banned the craft from my home this past year. It has been the source of great pain and despair to me, and the cause for my separation from my wife. If you think me harsh for having Saghani hanged for being a witch when she saved my life, then know I did not want to be saved. I wanted to join my daughter, my beloved Elsopeth, my 'Sophie' as I called her. I wanted to leave this earth. And thus, I condemn all that practice it.

In the last year of my marriage, I would not allow my wife to practice her witchery, nor do I believe it should be practised. I am a crusader for abolishing this abhorrent custom. It favours some and not others, no different to offering prayer when some are blessed and others are not. It could not save my Sophie from illness and I watched her die before reaching her tenth year. What good is it to say you have the gift when God can still call back his children at any time?

Do you know what it is to love a witch? At first, I found her intriguing, mystical and so different from anyone I had ever met. A great beauty she was, and for a young man new to the village, I was flattered that she would even glance my way. I heard she was considered a prize. Her hair was silver-white, her skin like porcelain and her eyes were pale blue. I could not breathe around her for her beauty. She had a delicate charm and a soft laugh. It was not long until we wed.

But then I wondered if she had charmed me to marry her. If she was so loved and admired as I heard, why had no one else asked for her hand? I was determined to be open in our marriage and I asked her. She assured me she waited for me, had foreseen my arrival and of course I was happy to accept that story. The first years of our marriage passed with blissful happiness – a time of discovery and love. I worked hard, we built a home, and I loved to come home to her.

But on one occasion as I left the tavern having shared an ale with a colleague, I heard a stranger to town comment to his friend about a woman so fearfully ugly she must be a witch. I found great amusement in the comment and when I turned to see whom he spoke of, the only woman opposite on the street was my wife who had come to walk with me home. I thought perhaps he said it in jest but then I began to wonder... did I really see the woman who was my wife, or was I seeing this magical fairy-like creature, and those not bewitched by her, saw something else again. It frightened me.

I found myself trying to see her reflection on surfaces, to see if I could catch her out. I woke at night to glance at her face but it always appeared the same, beautiful, delicate face. Then our daughter, Sophie, was born, and she too had the look of her mother with her pale blue eyes and ivory skin, but unlike her mother's silver hair, she had golden locks.

For a while, I forgot my fears. In our happiness, it didn't seem important, until yet again I saw the reaction of a stranger to Issbelle when we ventured from our small farm into the village. Was Sophie like her mother? Was she some frightening changeling I could not truly see?

And so, I asked around, but no one would tell me. I was told "I had nothing to fear" or "beauty is in the eyes of the beholder" or "with love and family, we are all prejudiced in our views." I stopped asking. Either magic had prevented them from telling me the truth or they could not see her real form either. Or, they were too frightened to speak against my witch wife.

When Sophie became ill, I was despairing. We could not save my beloved golden girl despite the many people Issbelle healed daily, or the magic she used to make our life prosperous. She blamed me as Sophie was half me – non-magical – and half her mother. I blamed her for healing everyone but the one person who represented our love.

I left. She did not bewitch me to return, and I am grateful for that. But I had lost the will to live. When I found out that a witch had saved me, I was enraged. I never wish to have any dealings with the charmed people again.

To think the accursed Saghani has inflicted the sight on me so that when I put on my seeing glasses to read, I see futures before me, speaks of their treachery. I am sorry her husband and sons have lost her in their life but it is time that these people are destroyed.

I heard Issbelle resurrected a spirit of our daughter who lives with her and provides comfort. Let the child rest in peace. Let me rest in peace as well.

*****

Lukas sat back from the book and closed his eyes. He had forgotten the daughter's nickname was Sophie. He had no reason to remember it when he did not know Sophie then. The golden-haired daughter of a witch in the 16th century who did not survive but in spirit form, shares her namesake with Sophie in the 21st century – the clairvoyant who Daphne believed would be the most powerful of them all.

Chapter 16

Cassie Delaney's sister, Kim Parsons, was no beauty, not even a makeover would help. Gerard was right, Sophie thought. Kim hadn't been a beauty in her younger years, and she had not improved with time. Sophie glanced Gerard's way, and he raised an eyebrow at her in a *told you so* fashion.

Sophie could understand if Kim resented her beautiful sister, Cassie – without Cassie around, Kim's life might have been quite different. She may not have been constantly compared to her younger sister. She might have been accepted for who she was, judged for her achievements, not her appearance, and ultimately not tainted by Cassie's murder. But that was not Kim's childhood experience.

They sat around the kitchen table in a neat and small house, which seemed smaller as Kim had covered every inch of the surface with clutter – cooking books, canisters, cups, photos, ornaments – there was barely a spot spare. It reminded Sophie of Aunt Daphne's office when she had taken over it. Sophie hated clutter.

'So why are you dragging this up again?' she asked. 'It's been what, thirty years?'

'It has indeed, Mrs Parsons,' Gerard said.

'Call me Kim.'

Sophie had the glasses perched on her head for now, but she was watching Kim study Gerard and then it dawned on Kim. 'Oh my God, you're the detective from the original investigation. Wow, still around?'

'Apparently,' he said with little humour in his voice and she chuckled.

'Good, I don't have to go back over my story,' she said, carrying a coffee pot to the dining room table and sitting down with them. Sophie pushed the cups forward as Kim poured and distributed them. 'I have to confess I don't remember much of it now.'

'Happens to the best of us,' Gerard said and she chuckled again.

'Maybe I could just ask some questions and you could give me a brief response? That would be helpful,' Sophie suggested.

Kim studied her and nodded. 'You're that clairvoyant, aren't you? I saw you rescued the little girl, that was something.'

'It was a huge relief, and I nearly blew it,' Sophie said and exhaled.

'How did you nearly blow it?' Kim asked.

'I almost missed the nephew; he was leaving when I arrived.' She wanted to over-share with Kim. Sophie sensed Kim was the type who preferred down-to-earth people, who called a spade-a-spade. Besides, Sophie could relax more with Gerard and say what she thought. She didn't have to be so public relations minded about maintaining the police force's image; he wasn't, after all.

'Crap, what would have happened then if he'd left?' Kim asked out of curiosity.

'I don't know. I often have to see people connected to a person or incident to read them. It's why I wear the glasses so I see them closer,' she said explaining as she pulled the glasses down from her head and put them on.

Kim took a bite of the cake Sophie had brought with them and spoke with her mouth half full. 'Geez, you're out of luck now then aren't you, given Cassie's been dead 30 years? She's going to be hard to see.'

'Doesn't help,' Sophie said and made Kim laugh.

'Fire away,' Kim invited her. 'Ask anything you like.'

Sophie saw the look of surprise on Gerard's face.

'You never gave me an inch!' he exclaimed.

'I didn't like you,' Kim said and then chuckled. Gerard shook his head and smiled at her. Time had mellowed them both.

'But did you like her, Cassie?' Sophie asked.

Kim's eyes widened with surprise and she took a mouthful of coffee before answering. 'You know, no one has ever asked me that. They just assumed because I was the ugly sister that I was jealous of Cassie and hateful, happy to have her gone. But I wasn't.'

Sophie watched the small images appearing around Kim as she spoke of her little sister. She was speaking the truth.

'There were three of us – I was the eldest, then my brother, Myles, and Cassie was the baby. She was like a doll. I wanted to hate her, but I couldn't.'

'Why?' Gerard asked.

'Because she loved me.'

Sophie smiled, moved, and a little melancholy. What she would have given for a sister or a brother.

Kim continued: 'Dad never got over Cassie's disappearance, it drove him to an early grave. Mum is still looking for her, and I married and got out as quickly as I could. Everyone knew our name, and I got sick of being asked about it or being a suspect,' she said with a glance to Gerard.

He gave a nod and a small shrug of apology.

'It doesn't matter. I've had a good life. My husband and I have been married for over twenty-five years, we've got three good kids and six grandkids. That's alright.'

'That's great,' Sophie said. 'Did you ever have an inkling of what happened? Who might have been involved?' Sophie ciphered through the images above and around Kim.

Kim shook her head. 'Her boyfriend was a muso and he was a nice guy, wasn't he?' she asked Gerard.

'Yeah, he was alright. He was playing in the band at Cassie's birthday party most of the night, and had plenty of eyes on him – his alibi was watertight,' Gerard said.

'My brother and I, and my husband who was my boyfriend then, all left the party before Cassie went missing, so there were sightings of her alive after we left.'

'Do you remember anyone at the party who shouldn't have been there? Gate-crashers or any shady characters?' Sophie asked. Again, Kim's images showed no threats or clues. Just people hugging, dancing, talking…

'No, we knew everyone. It wasn't a huge gathering, maybe fifty or so at home. Cassie was hanging out with her fellow beauty queen friends most of the night and they were as thick as thieves. Miss Charity, Miss Personality, Miss Beauty Runner-up, Miss Lord-Knows-What,' she brushed it off. 'My brother married Miss Beauty Runner-up, Kate. Those girls would not let anything happen to each other; they'd known each other for years. So, Mum and I were pretty convinced that Cassie left her birthday party with someone else, either by force or by trickery.'

'Thank you, Kim,' Sophie said and took the glasses off. She looked to Gerard who gave her a surprised look that she was finished so soon.

'It'd be good if you found something,' Kim said. 'Dad's gone and is probably with Cassie looking down on us from Heaven now, and knows the truth. But it'd be nice for Mum to know after all these years.'

'I'll give it my best, I assure you,' Sophie said. 'Besides Gerard wants to retire and not think about it every day.'

'Wow! Is it really still on your radar?' Kim turned to face him. 'I've heard of cops who have the one that gets away.'

'Cassie is mine, haunts me,' Gerard said in a rare show of emotion. 'And it annoys the shit out of me that I can't close it.'

'Best get to it then,' Kim said with a wink to Sophie.

*****

'Well, you won her over,' Gerard said after he had driven them some distance down the street.

'Like I won you over?' Sophie joked and Gerard chuckled.

'Yeah, keep working at it.' He gave her a wink. He liked the clairvoyant; she was sassy and she put up with his grumpiness without trying to redeem him. But he wasn't going to admit that to Murdoch. She was easy on the eye as well. 'You didn't ask her much.'

'Didn't need to. It's like you said, she's not involved, there was no death around her.'

'I'm kind of pleased,' Gerard said. 'She had it tough during those years, everyone suspicious of her. It was cruel in retrospect.'

'Sure was,' Sophie agreed. 'So, who next?'

'You tell me and I'll set it up in the next few days. Don't worry, I'll check with your security guard, Miss Sharpe, first for the best day and time. How about the brother?'

Sophie chuckled at his reference to Miss Sharpe. 'The brother and his wife, I think – Miss Beauty Runner-up, together if we can,' she said.

'Let's see how Miss Beauty Runner-up fared with the years,' Gerard said.

'Hopefully as good as you,' Sophie said, and he glanced away from the road long enough to give her a smirk as she laughed at her own joke.

Chapter 17

A large vintage cream-coloured Jaguar was parked in the visitors' allocated parking area when Sophie arrived at the office in Daphne's grand home on Serendipity Lane the next morning. She wondered which charity group was hosting the driver who clearly could afford to be a benefactor. Miss Sharpe's sensible small car was there and Sophie parked next to it.

She had long hoped to be bequeathed the grand old home, in all its disrepair, but it was not to be. Aunt Daphne's solicitor Mr Saggers of Saggers & Son – a man who looked as if he had just stepped out of a Dickens' novel – announced that Sophie's Aunt Virginia got the contents of the cellar, her cousin Rupert or Brad as he preferred to be known, scored the Rolls Royce, and just when she thought she was on the home straight, Mr Saggers announced that the grand old home in Serendipity Lane was to be used by some health and harmony groups managed by a board and blah, blah, blah. Aunt Daphne had bequeathed Sophie the glasses – and she had no knowledge of their power or how they would change her life.

She walked up the path to the imposing residence that heralded from the past century when servants had their own quarters and a footman and butler greeted you at the door. There were wings for guests, and rooms that overlooked the parks and gardens that once sprawled over half the neighbourhood. The land around Aunt Daphne's home had also been subdivided over the years but the building still sat on what was equivalent to four normal house blocks, and included a long driveway to the entrance way, and lovely gardens maintained by her will with a perpetuity clause.

Like Aunt Daphne, the house was a grand old dame and the prestigious Jaguar out the front was a delightful throwback to its glory days. Its grandeur always took Sophie in. She could imagine herself sweeping around the house and gardens in a large puffy-Victorian dress, accepting gentleman callers. For a moment she imagined Murdoch and Lukas in their Victorian finery coming to call – tall and striking in their frock coats, waistcoats and gloves. She sighed at the lovely thought and entered the office area of her clairvoyant business, where the plush rugs, chairs and curtains looked so inviting and the light coming through the bay windows gave everything a pleasant glow.

'Good morning, Miss Sharpe,' she called only to find Miss Sharpe right behind her. That was not an uncommon occurrence.

'Sophie, good morning, dear, we have a guest,' Miss Sharpe said and indicated Mr Saggers taking tea at the table by the bay window where a large teapot and several cups, a milk jug, and sugar bowl rested, implying a meeting was imminent. It was as if Sophie had conjured him with her thoughts.

'Here is the young lady herself,' Mr Saggers said rising.

'Mr Saggers! Good to see you again.' Sophie moved towards him to greet the senior solicitor from Saggers & Son. The devastation she felt after that meeting when he read out Aunt Daphne's will and intentions was still fresh but her acceptance was absolute.

Mr Saggers rose to shake her hand and also gave a small bow, charming and old fashioned. It suited the strange old fellow as Daphne once described him; Sophie found him a little on the creepy side.

Miss Sharpe spoke up: 'Mr Saggers has some news about Daphne's will if you would like to be seated, Sophie, and perhaps take tea?'

'I'll pour, Miss Sharpe. Please do take a seat as well.' Sophie sat finding she always became more formal in her speech around Miss Sharpe.

'If you insist, that would be lovely,' Miss Sharpe said, pleased to be part of the meeting of which, Sophie had no doubt, she already knew the subject and content.

'Is that your beautiful Jaguar, Mr Saggers?' Sophie asked.

'My pride and joy,' he said looking out across the lawn to the car park where he could see his cream-coloured vintage car. 'A 1961 Mark II, quite a classic.'

'Beautiful,' Sophie said again. Putting aside the car, Sophie returned her attention to Mr Saggers. She had never seen a straighter nose on a man who had curves everywhere else. She could use it as a ruler.

Mr Saggers cleared his throat. 'I am here because there is a codicil to Mrs Daphne Shelby's will.'

'What does that mean, Mr Saggers?' Sophie asked.

'It's like an extra note that Daphne wanted to have acted upon, in this case, at a later date than the first reading of the will,' Miss Sharpe said.

'Precisely,' Mr Saggers said, giving Miss Sharpe a nod.

'Another directive from Great Aunt Daphne from the other side!' Sophie said, looking skyward. She dropped her gaze to Mr Saggers. 'Goodness, do you want the glasses back?' she asked alarmed, thinking of what she had given up and been through thus far.

'No, no, definitely not,' he assured her holding up his hand and Miss Sharpe smiled like a Cheshire cat – something mysterious was definitely on the meeting's agenda. He explained: 'Because of a condition which you have now fulfilled, the original will has changed.'

'Oh, really. I didn't know that could be done.'

'Shall I read it to you?' Mr Saggers asked.

'Yes, please,' Sophie said, keen to move the man along and to get to work. She wanted to check her emails, prepare for her readings today, and do some research on Cassie Delaney's brother and Cassie's fellow beauty queens. She was also keen to drop in on Lukas at the *Optical Illusion* store, and see if she could get her family's witching history without all the glass breaking like last time. The thought of Lukas brought Lucy to mind and a small stab of pain hit her heart; she had not heard from her friend despite leaving several messages.

Mr Saggers reached down and opened a leather briefcase that sat on the floor leaning against his chair. He pulled out a small document and taking a pair of thin, silver framed spectacles from his coat pocket, he slid them onto his straight nose and hooked them behind his ears. Sophie remembered the ceremony last time at the will reading and sipped her tea, waiting patiently. Miss Sharpe maintained a pleasant look as if expecting good news.

Sophie mused; Aunt Daphne's probably got a psychic hairbrush she wants to give me now. She bit her lip to stop from chuckling.

Mr Saggers cleared his throat and read from the document. 'This is the instruction from Mrs Daphne Shelby: "It is my wish and desire that when my niece, Miss Sophie Carell, formally announces that she will follow in my footsteps and continue with my clients and police work in her capacity as a clairvoyant, and advises this decision to Miss Valerie Sharpe, I bequeath Sophie my house and grounds, knowing she will do the right thing by her community tenants". So be it.'

Sophie's mouth dropped open as Miss Sharpe gave a clap and a small cry of delight. Mr Saggers permitted himself a smile as he folded his glasses and put them back in his pocket.

Sophie sat frozen until Miss Sharpe touched her arm and she blinked and turned to Miss Sharpe.

'Oh my God, Miss Sharpe, did you know? Of course you knew. I am now the owner of this beautiful home... and the grounds... and the offices?'

'You are my dear,' Miss Sharpe said, excited for her.

'May I offer my congratulations?' Mr Saggers said.

'Thank you,' Sophie said stunned. 'I need time to process this. It's too mind-blowing, too much...'

Miss Sharpe nodded wisely. 'And that is why you now

have earned it, because you can see a real purpose for your life and this house. Well done, Sophie, well done.'

Sophie's thoughts went to the tenants – to Melino and her sports groups, and the smattering of other tenants reliant on the space.

'It's so mind-blowing,' Sophie said, still stunned as Mr Saggers finished his tea and Miss Sharpe continued to smile.

'Will you be keeping the other businesses operating in the west wing?' Mr Saggers asked.

Sophie could feel Miss Sharpe's observation of her. She knows, Sophie was sure of it.

'Of course I will, there's plenty of room for us all here.'

Miss Sharpe exhaled, no doubt happy to hear Sophie say the words and confirm it.

'My nephew, Nikolas, will make an appointment to see you and discuss the books which have been his responsibility now for many years,' Mr Saggers said with a serious countenance as if to ensure Sophie knew they took their responsibility very seriously. He continued: 'The community groups pay a nominal rent which covers your rates, insurance and garden maintenance. You will need to set aside a certain amount to maintain the house, including your amenities if you move in. Nikolas will be happy to help you with all that.'

'Wonderful, thank you, Mr Saggers.' Sophie wondered if Nikolas, the nephew, would be as ancient as his uncle and if the son of Saggers & Son actually existed.

'You can move in from today if you like,' Mr Saggers continued. 'It is all legal.'

'Move in. Oh right, of course, there's the rest of the house,' she said with a glance out the side window to the next wing.

'It might require a little cleanout, dear,' Miss Sharpe suggested. 'Your aunt, as you may recall was a bit of a bowerbird.'

'Miss Sharpe she was a dreadful hoarder, you are being kind,' Sophie said and laughed.

Miss Sharpe laughed along. 'Yes, that's probably a more apt description. Well then, I suggest you accept the keys and take a tour. Detective Ashcroft will arrive in a moment and he might like to accompany you. Just in case anything has dislodged itself,' she said as if that might happen.

'Do I have an appointment with Murdoch?' Sophie asked as she saw his car come up the driveway.

'No, he's just dropping in I imagine to find out how you went with Detective Oakley.'

Sophie gave Miss Sharpe a suspicious look. 'There's not much that gets past you, Miss Sharpe.'

'Oh, I wouldn't say that,' she said modestly. 'I'll see Mr Saggers out if you see Detective Ashcroft in.'

'Deal,' Sophie said, and accepting the keys from Mr Saggers with her thanks, she smiled again in delight at Miss Sharpe as she held the keys to her chest. She just had to wait now for Murdoch who she saw through the bay window had stopped to admire the Jaguar. This might take some time.

Chapter 18

Lukas had the morning off work. It was in exchange for the evening he worked during the week keeping *Optical Illusion* opened for late trading hours, like other retailers on the street. He was due to start at midday today and with a glance at the clock, he had a few hours up his sleeve.

'Do you think we should get up?' Lucy asked lying beside him in bed, her head resting in the crook of his arm. She had no modelling shoots booked today or tomorrow.

He kissed the top of her head. 'Thinking about it.'

She ran her fingers over the marks on his torso. 'These are fresh bruises,' she said and leaned over to study his skin.

'They're nothing, don't worry about it.'

'But how did you get them? You avoided the subject last time I asked. Don't think I didn't notice,' Lucy said looking up at him.

'That doesn't sound like me,' he said and made her laugh. He pulled himself up further on the pillow, taking Lucy with him. 'I was training, I am training, just to keep fit, a form of martial arts.'

'But these are burn marks over here,' she said touching a scar, and he flinched.

'We play rough,' he assured her.

'Okay, so you don't want to talk about it, I get it,' she said and sighed.

Lukas looked to the ceiling, trying to come up with some explanation or to reveal something that would satisfy Lucy. How could he explain he was trying to cast aside a hovering fireball of anger that his grandfather was intending to send back his way? He exhaled.

'I'm getting up,' she said, and he reached over quickly and pulled her back.

'Wait, Lucy, wait up.'

She rolled her eyes, lay back down on her stomach and putting her chin in her hands, gave him her full attention.

'I'm sorry if I'm not the most open person. I'm not deliberately keeping things from you,' he said, looking at her with sincerity, 'and I'm not doing anything that would risk our relationship or hurt you. Trust me.'

'Trust you?' she asked, exasperated. 'Lukas, your closed-book ways will be the thing that breaks us up.'

'Really?' he frowned surprised. He spread his hands out in a frustrated gesture. 'Ask me what you want to know and I'll try to answer.'

'What do you think of me?'

He smiled. 'Well, that's easy, I love you.'

'More or less?' she asked.

Lukas frowned, confused at the question. 'You want a sliding scale? What do I compare my love to? A summer's day?' he quoted Shakespeare.

'See this is what I mean,' she sat up and crossed her legs in front of her. 'I've had exes who tell me they can't live without me, or that they can't imagine life without me, or that I'm their greatest love…'

'But now they're exes,' he pointed out.

'You're just making fun of this.'

'I'm not. I'm sorry, let me give you some context.' He thought for a moment. 'Okay, well this is one of the two most significant relationships I've ever had, and I'm completely in love with you and committed to you.' He said and looked to Lucy hoping that would satisfy her.

'Hmm, be still my beating heart, so romantic,' she said.

Lukas's lips thinned with frustration and anger.

'Why does Sophie have to be in your life?' Lucy asked, and Lukas chuckled then realised she was serious.

'She's one of your closest friends,' he reminded her.

'Yes, but not yours. Why do you have to spend time with her every time she visits the store?'

'You know about her glasses; she's trusted that to you. I'm her contact… every beholder of every generation has one.' He tried to make it sound uncomplicated.

'The whole thing is weird. I don't want you to be her *contact*. Why can't Alfred or Orli look after her?' Lucy said.

'Because Alfred was Daphne's contact, and he wants to retire. Orli, well it's not her thing.'

Lucy shrugged. 'So why does it have to be your thing? How would you like it if I was always working with a good-looking guy every day?'

'You are,' he said. 'You work with male models, photographers, designers, make-up people all day every day. I have to suck it up.'

107

'That's different. I'm not close to them and you don't know them. You're hanging around with one of my closest friends who is beautiful and clever. I'm not an idiot... a spark is going to light.'

'A spark is not going to light,' Lukas said getting weary of the conversation. 'I'm holding a huge flame for you, that's how it compares.'

He watched as she thought on his answer for a moment and hoped that would satisfy her. But no.

'Well, we all have to make sacrifices for our relationships and if we are going to go the distance, that's what I want. I don't want you to be Sophie's contact.'

With that, she stood and headed to her shower. Lukas fell back onto the pillows.

What the hell do I do now?

He closed his eyes and sought his grandfather. He felt the buzz in his temple – he thought about Lucy's ultimatum so his grandfather could hear his thought and prepare. They'd talk at midday.

*****

Murdoch opened a door to one of the large rooms on the ground floor of Aunt Daphne's house and declared it 'clear'.

'Clear of what?' Sophie asked. 'Ghosts, birds, Aunt Daphne?'

'All that, but not dust,' he said, coughing as he opened a curtain and the dust swirled around him. 'Great view.'

Sophie joined him at the window and looked out over the gardens to the distant wall and gates. 'I can't believe I own this; I can't get my head around it.'

'Makes you a reasonably good catch,' he joked, and she hit his arm playfully. 'Unless the rates, maintenance, gardening fees and so on send you broke.'

'Then I'll need to find a handy boyfriend. Put him to work,' she said, pleased with the suggestion.

'Poor bastard,' Murdoch said, and gave her a grin. He brushed the dust from his grey suit.

'Hold off on dusting yourself down just yet, there's another floor.'

They heard a noise upstairs and Sophie raised an eyebrow in Murdoch's direction.

'I hope that's just a possum and not a squatter I have to move out,' he grumbled at the thought of having to become heavy-handed.

'I'd prefer a squatter,' Sophie said, wrinkling her nose.

They moved through several rooms, admiring some of Aunt Daphne's statues and furniture. 'I love this fireplace, not that we'd have much use for it ten months of the year.'

'I love the art déco plaster features on the walls and ceilings,' Murdoch said looking up. 'You're lucky they are in pretty good nick. It'd be a killer to restore them.'

'I didn't pick you for a plaster guy,' she teased.

'I'm many things, including plaster,' he assured her. 'So, I heard you got on pretty well with my partner,' he said as they made their way up the large winding timber staircase.

Sophie flashed Murdoch a grin. 'We had a good time actually, he's alright. He can take a joke.'

'Yeah? Can't say we laugh much. But you're better looking than me, that probably helps,' Murdoch said.

'No doubt,' she agreed. 'You know, this staircase was the

biggest thing in the world when I was a kid visiting Aunt Daphne. I thought it went on forever.' Sophie ran her hand up the dark timber banister. They got to the top of the staircase and stopped.

'Left or right?' Murdoch asked looking down the hallway with closed doors on both sides.

They heard the noise again to the left, down the end of the hallway in the front room. Murdoch moved in front of Sophie and made his way along the hall, she stayed close behind. He opened the door and reeled back. Sophie yelped in fright. The window was open and a dozen or more large black ravens were in the room.

Murdoch strode in and they rose around him, as if in unison and went straight for the window, flying out one after the other. He looked around ensuring none were remaining and closed the window. He turned back to Sophie.

'The Raven,' she whispered, and their eyes locked.

Chapter 19

Lukas jumped out of bed and hurriedly threw on his jeans and the black polo shirt he had arrived in last night. His runners were on in minutes and his gear stuffed into his bag. He stopped and waited. He had sensed danger, something lurking near Sophie, something she was about to encounter. Now, the feeling wasn't gone, but it wasn't as clear or strong.

Lucy appeared from the shower; a towel wrapped around her.

'That was quick. Not showering?'

'I'll go home and change before work,' he said, keen to get to his car to read the signal clearer. He didn't want to run out on Lucy given their recent discussion, but he wanted to be prepared. 'I'd better run. Call you later?'

'Sure,' she said and accepted his kiss. 'Are you angry about the Sophie thing?'

'No, I'll work it out. Thanks for last night, and this morning.' He quickly kissed her again, concerned that he might have to orb in her presence and be momentarily in the two places at once. It drained him to do it and Lucy wouldn't notice physically but he would be half there and half concentrating. Again, it was something his grandfather and Orli both did better. He was becoming very aware of his shortcomings.

He was out of Lucy's townhouse and in his car in moments. Lukas drove a street away, out of sight and pulled the car over to the footpath, cutting the ignition. Closing his eyes, he waited, trying to read the situation. It was a weak pull, but something wasn't right.

With deep concentration, he left his body and physically appeared behind Sophie. She was following the detective, Murdoch Ashcroft, down a hallway towards a door... he opened it and she gasped. Lukas was right behind her as she saw the ravens. The dark, menacing birds rose and, through the open window, left the room. Murdoch, the raven, turned around to face them.

*****

'Tell your protector to stand down,' Murdoch said, his dark eyes glaring with intent, his body tense with anticipation.

'Protector?' Sophie said and whirled around to find Lukas behind her.

'Lukas. Where did you come from?' she asked, wide-eyed and looking up at Lukas Lens.

'I'm not here, in body,' he said, not taking his eyes off Murdoch.

'I won't hurt her,' Murdoch said, and held up his hands. 'I assure you, she is safe with me.'

Lukas looked to Sophie then back to Murdoch and reading the situation, faded, his image disappearing. Frowning, Sophie turned back to Murdoch.

'Murdoch! What is going on?'

His eyes narrowed, and he said nothing as he tried to determine if she knew he was the raven.

'Right,' she said almost in a whisper, as they held each other's gaze.

'You know, about Lukas, the raven and—' she started.

'Of course I know,' he cut her off. 'So do you then?'

'Yes. But you knew you were the raven all the years you worked with Aunt Daphne? You knew you were our enemy?' Sophie stepped back toward the door.

Murdoch frowned as he read her fear. 'I'm not going to hurt you, Sophie. I've had plenty of opportunities to do that and never touched a hair on your head. Nor did I ever hurt your Great Aunt. Besides, *enemy* is a little strong.'

'Not if you read the diary entries I've read.'

He stepped towards her and she stepped back again. Murdoch sighed.

'I'm a cop. I swore to protect. We've been in the car together for hours on end. I've been to your house. I saved you from my murderous ex-girlfriend!'

'You're the raven!' Sophie pointed out the obvious. 'Lukas is the dove. I'm… well I'm the one who started it all, or rather my ancestor did. I can understand a generational grudge,' she said warily.

'There was more to it than that.' Again, Murdoch studied her – she did not appear to know a lot about their shared history, yet. He reassured her again: 'Trust me, if I wanted to hurt you I could do so in a second.' With that, he was at her side instantly and she yelped in fright. Lukas appeared and shoved Murdoch away. He stumbled back a few steps and arced up, a wall of strength.

Two ravens appeared, tapping on the windowsill and glared in at the inhabitants of the room.

'I told you I am not going to hurt her,' Murdoch growled, 'I was just proving a point.'

Lukas faded again and Murdoch smiled.

'He's not strong enough for you yet. But in time, he will be.' Murdoch turned to the window and nodded; the ravens rose and flew away as if given permission.

'Lukas and I are both new in our roles, if you can call them that. I'm learning and Lukas is trying to help me without rushing me,' she said, defending him.

'Don't worry, I'm not going to test him unless he provokes me to do so.'

Sophie's eyes narrowed with annoyance. 'You are playing cat and mouse. On one hand you say you are not going to hurt me, but on the other you are making fun of the man who tries to protect me.'

Murdoch lowered himself onto the windowsill. 'Consider me reprimanded and humble.' He gave a small bow of his head as if conceding a tournament. 'You don't know the full story, do you?' he quirked his head on the side, like a raven, his dark eyes trying to penetrate her thoughts.

'I know there is more to my witching side of the family but Lukas prevented me from reading it last time I asked to see it, he's protecting me.'

'You don't sound convinced of that. Might be a good time

to rub this incident in his face, even if he tried to protect you just now. What has he told you?'

Sophie cleared her throat and tried not to sound defensive. 'A lot already. It's been a big learning curve these past few months… but I'm not completely across everything.'

'He's protecting you and feeding you incrementally,' Murdoch said, his chin up. And then he surprised her. 'He's right, I'd do the same thing.'

Sophie sighed. 'Oh good, because I need more men in my life telling me what to do and when I need it.'

Murdoch chuckled and Sophie relaxed a little.

'C'mon, let's finish the tour,' he said, rising from the windowsill and brushing the back of his suit pants.

She threw her hands up in the air in frustration. 'What? That's it? You tell me you know you are the raven and then let's have a cup of tea?'

'A cup of tea would be welcomed,' he said and smiled. 'Your protector is right. There's no hurry, we've got a lifetime.'

Sophie made her way to the door. 'He has a name you know.'

'He does, but you don't know it,' Murdoch said.

'Lukas,' Sophie said, 'not some silly witching name you've all given each other.'

Murdoch chuckled again.

'Come then and I shall make us both a cup of tea and I might even find a biscuit for you if you are lucky.'

'Fortunate me,' Murdoch said, following her out of the room and down the impressive stairwell.

'You and I, Sophie, we have met before, you know,' he softly whispered in her ear, the words full of intent in his baritone voice.

Sophie turned sharply on the stairs to ward him off, almost losing her balance, but he wasn't close by like she thought. Murdoch reached out and grabbed for her, straightening Sophie and waiting until her hand was on the rail before releasing her.

'Thank you,' she mumbled. 'What do you mean? As in a past life? Is that what you are talking about?'

They entered the kitchen and Murdoch looked out the window as Sophie prepared tea.

'Yes, in a past life. In many past lives. You and I go way back.'

'Do Lukas and I go way back?'

'No. He's a relatively young soul, not like us.'

Sophie raised an eyebrow in his direction. 'So let me understand this. The ever-pragmatic, often sullen, Detective Murdoch Ashcroft believes in reincarnation and has wooed me in past centuries?'

The kettle boiled, and she made their tea as Murdoch grinned at her and retorted: 'I didn't say I had wooed you.'

'Oh,' she said and genuinely looked embarrassed, which Sophie rarely was in male company.

'But yes, I wooed you,' he added, and she rolled her eyes at him. 'If you believe in reincarnation, then our souls are reborn from the past in human, animal or spirit form.'

'So, I may have been a cat and you could have been my human,' she teased, placing the tea on the table.

'I assure you I did not woo you or anyone else in animal form unless I was the same, of course. But we have travelled together before, many times.'

Sophie frowned, thinking of his words. Finding some

of Miss Sharpe's shortbread, which Miss Sharpe regularly supplied her with these days, she invited Murdoch to join her at the table.

'Has everyone in my life travelled with me before?'

'So they say if you believe in reincarnation.' Murdoch reached for a biscuit and took a bite. 'You travel with the same group of souls each time you are reincarnated, but what roles you play in each other's lives can differ.'

Sophie sighed, closed her eyes and thought for a moment before reopening them. 'It's all too much, sometimes.'

'It doesn't have to be,' he said with a shrug. 'We have no control over it anyway, so enjoy the ride.'

'You are always so laid back. I wish I could be more so,' she said.

'A compliment! I think...'

Sophie grinned. 'Yeah, I'll give you that one.'

'This is going to be an interesting generation of witches – you, me and *Lukas*,' he said, accentuating the protector's name to show Sophie that he knew it. 'But don't be complacent, Sophie, it won't be without its challenges.'

She had a feeling in her heart and her stomach – where she felt all her stress – that Murdoch's warning was ominous and he wasn't talking about the future, but the now.

Chapter 20

Lukas Lens arrived at *Optical Illusion*, entering via the back exit from the carpark. There were several customers in the store and both Alfred and Orli served at the counter. He went to the small bathroom, splashed some water over his face and took a deep breath. Lukas hadn't gone home to change, deciding instead to work away from the public and stay out the back of the shop for the afternoon; Orli could book in the jobs for him at the front desk should he get any watch-related customers. He felt grateful for the few moments to gather himself before he faced the barrage of questions from his family. It took all of twenty minutes until the store was cleared and Alfred and Orli joined him.

'Couldn't find a razor today, lad,' Alfred teased him and Lukas smiled.

'It's been a shocker of a morning,' he said and swore under his breath.

'Lukas!' Orli exclaimed, and he apologised.

'That's alright,' Alfred smiled. 'I've sworn myself under extreme aggravation. On one particularly stressful occasion, I said "bloody hell" twice in one morning.'

Orli laughed at her uncle. 'I can't imagine it,' she teased him. Turning to Lukas she added: 'We are here for you, Lukas, when you are ready to talk.'

Lukas exhaled and relaxed a little. The tension wasn't there that he expected from his grandfather and cousin, Orli. They were both very relaxed and at ease. He was the one feeling like he was walking on shifting sand but their centredness calmed him.

He cleared his throat and admitted: 'I'm no way near prepared or ready to protect Sophie,' he said, disappointed in himself.

'I take my share of responsibility for that, Lukas,' Alfred said, making a pot of tea for three and placing the cups on a tray. He flicked the kettle on and spooned tea leaves into a large, ceramic pot. 'My father drove me to achieve his benchmarks in skill levels, but your father was not here to demand that of you, and I have been lapse in my duty.'

'No, Grandpa, you haven't. I showed very little interest, I know you tried,' Lukas said with regret. 'I was too interested in rebelling and doing my own thing.'

'It was a difficult time for you when your parents died. Difficult for all of us,' Alfred conceded thinking on the loss of his son, Mendel, and daughter-in-law, Freya.

'I'm surprised you didn't send me away to boarding school,' Lukas said. They had never spoken of that time in any great depth, just skimmed over it, avoiding the pain and conflict.

Orli looked at Lukas sympathetically. 'I was eight, you must have been thirteen? I remember Mum and Dad were so devastated, especially Dad to have lost his beloved cousin.'

'The boys had grown up together and were very close,' Alfred agreed.

'You got expelled from school, didn't you, Lukas?' Orli asked.

Lukas frowned. 'That was the tip of the iceberg. You never told anyone, Grandpa?'

'Why would I, lad? We got through it.'

Lukas scoffed and turned to Orli. 'I decided to punish Grandpa and Daphne because they knew it was going to happen and did nothing.'

Orli gasped. 'Uncle Alfred, no! How did you learn?'

'I found out in the early days in my role as protector to Daphne. My fault... asking too many questions, Daphne was a little careless too, and it slipped that my boy and daughter-in-law were to die. I was devastated and could do nothing to prevent it,' he said, and stopped momentarily as his voice hitched. Orli moved quickly to him and embraced him, Lukas looked away, ashamed.

'Mendel was the only child we were blessed with and he was with us until he married with his own child – I would have gladly traded my life for theirs in a heartbeat.'

Lukas swallowed his emotion and blinked back tears, surprised by how quickly the pain resurfaced, as if the years in between did not exist.

'It was the waiting that was so excruciating,' Alfred said, sharing more of his past than usual. 'Knowing and waiting for the day to come when I would lose him, and lovely Freya. Knowing what that what do to you, Lukas.'

'And I made your life more miserable,' Lukas said. He turned to Orli. 'I was angry at Grandpa and Daphne, so I burnt down the house.'

120

Orli's hand flew to her mouth, her eyes wide with shock.

Lukas looked away. 'I also went joyriding in Grandpa's car and wrote it off, broke every window in the lower level of Daphne's house, and in this store while Grandpa was working behind the counter. There were more incidents, but that's the highlights.'

Alfred chuckled and Lukas looked up and gave him a sheepish smile.

'Well, lad,' he said, 'I've always said if you do something, do it well.'

Orli laughed and released her uncle from her arms. He placed an affectionate kiss on her head.

'But, it's my excuse for not training you well,' Alfred said. 'Then, I wasn't convinced we should continue the ancestral relationship. After losing Mendel, I wanted no part of it.' He said to Orli: 'Your father, Chauncey, felt the same.'

'Dad never told me that,' Orli said in contemplation of her father's thoughts on the family's witching past.

'I didn't want my brother, or his son, Chauncey, or either of you to ever know that pain. It took me a long time to come around.'

'Understandably,' Orli said, pouring the tea that Alfred had made and serving the three of them. 'So, what was Dad suggesting?'

'Chauncey thought we should continue, but it took him some time to come to that decision too.' Alfred sipped his tea and said: 'So Lukas, do you feel that as your powers are not well-enough developed, you should give up your role as Sophie's protector? Or will that serve as an excuse given Lucy's ultimatum of sorts?'

Lukas grimaced, yet again his grandfather had read him perfectly. He shook his head in the negative. 'Sorry to invade your thoughts,' Lukas said, 'but I tried to send Lucy's ultimatum to you so you both might have time to discuss it and consider my, our, actions.'

'The protector role can be reassigned but you cannot then claim it back once it has gone,' Orli said. 'There are cases in our history where this has happened and once control is relinquished, it is gone for good.'

She sat opposite Lukas with her tea. Alfred agreed.

'I don't want to give it up,' Lukas said. 'I like Sophie, and I enjoy being part of our history and called for duty. But, there's Lucy.' A stab of pain hit him when he imagined life without her. He wasn't sure he could sacrifice Lucy for Sophie, or Sophie for Lucy. He hated being put in this position.

'It's an awful position,' Alfred agreed with him, reading his mind.

'Think on it carefully, Lukas,' Orli said. 'Especially given the consequences to your relationship. Sophie might fall in love and you don't want to regret having given up what might be the love of your life to protect Sophie, if you are alone.'

Lukas nodded. 'That's what I'm afraid of, but I'm disappointed that Lucy would ask this of me.'

'It's not surprising,' Alfred said. 'Lucy and Sophie are beautiful young women, and Lucy may feel insecure with the time and attention you give to Sophie. I'm sure quite a few young ladies would.'

'Thanks, Grandpa,' Lukas said appreciating his empathy.

'But that's not the biggest problem this morning. Did you not sense it?' he asked surprised.

Orli and Alfred looked at each and back to him.

'No,' Orli said, 'we can sense you are extremely stressed, but what has happened?'

'It's Sophie… the birds, the raven…' Lukas said, gathering his thoughts.

Alfred gasped. 'Only the assigned protector can feel the threat of the raven. It's started, hasn't it?'

Lukas nodded. 'He knows. Murdoch Ashcroft knows he is the raven.'

Chapter 21

A knock at Sophie's door broke her concentration as her appointment arrived for a reading. Lucy wandered in, dressed casually in a long red dress with strappy, flat gold sandals.

'Lucy,' Sophie said surprised and involuntarily smiled, but her friend did not look quite as happy to see her.

'Hi Sophie, I'm your next reading.'

Sophie froze. 'I can't—'

'I've pre-paid and consider me a client. Just give me the same reading you give to everyone else.' Lucy moved towards the small table with two chairs. 'Is this where you do the readings?' she asked, and sat when Sophie nodded. She placed her handbag down on the ground beside her. Sophie stood from behind her desk.

'Miss Sharpe wouldn't have booked you in,' Sophie said confused and with a glance to the entranceway hoping Miss Sharpe – who had left for the day and had gone to her Bridge game – might manifest.

'She didn't. I booked online and used my alias – Neroli

Barker. But you can call me Lucy,' she said, and smiled at her own joke.

'I've missed you, Luce. You haven't been returning my calls or messages,' Sophie moved to the small table and sat opposite her.

'I needed to cool down. You don't have your glasses with you.'

Sophie sighed. 'Why would you push me to do this? We've discussed it already.'

'Because I know you can tell me what choice I made and what my future looks like. I know with you, it will be correct and I don't want to make the wrong choice... I want to pick the man who will love me, be with me always and be loyal.'

'I'm not sure I can see all that. All I can see is who you pick and if you stay together or not.'

'If I ask the right questions you can,' Lucy said. 'You told me that yourself.'

Sophie conceded defeat. Disappointed but feeling trapped, she rose, got the glasses, returned, and sitting, slipped them on. 'Go ahead then, ask me questions.'

Lucy nodded and asked immediately. 'Will I marry Lukas?'

The images appeared around Lucy's head and Sophie studied them. She saw the same things she saw that very first time she placed the glasses on and sat in the company of her friends Lucy and Blain. That time she had no idea of the power of the glasses, or what she was seeing. The images showed Lucy signing a wedding register in her bridal dress. She saw yet again, that she wasn't at the wedding. The first time Sophie had seen this she couldn't understand why she wouldn't be part of her friend's wedding when they were so close. Now she knew. She was going to lose Lucy and probably Lukas. She saw the ultimatum that Lucy had already delivered. Her eyes widened in surprise and she pulled the glasses off.

'You asked Lukas to pick you or me? Why?'

'How would you feel if your boyfriend was hanging around me all the time?'

'Well, if you worked together – if he was a model or set dresser, or designer, photographer, hairdresser, whatever, I'd trust you both and understand. Lukas and I work together, more or less.'

'Yeah, well I'm worried about the more not the less,' Lucy said seriously.

Sophie laughed and then stopped. 'Really? Lukas could have asked me out, but he asked you. Now, of course he will choose you, he loves you.'

'Who am I going to marry, Sophie?' she asked again.

Sophie put the glasses back on but then a strange phenomenon happened. One that she hadn't experienced before – she couldn't see who the man was that Lucy was marrying.

'Ask me something about it again,' Sophie said. 'I can see you in a wedding dress but I can't see who the groom is.'

Lucy scoffed.

'This is weird… I need to ask Miss Sharpe. Ask me something related?' Sophie frowned.

Lucy asked a smattering of questions all related to romance, husband, wedding, engagement and groom but Sophie could not see her groom.

'I can't see the man… it'll sound weird but it's like there's a smudge where he should be. It's like those news stories where they blot out people.'

'You must be able to see something – his shape, hair colour, size?' Lucy demanded.

Sophie shook her head. 'I can see you and your mum, some girlfriends.'

'Well, I guess you won.'

'Lucy, I'm not doing it on purpose. I'm not seeing any men around you. Last time I saw Blain in the bridal party, but I can't see any men.'

'Right,' Lucy said unconvinced.

'Is it because I've seen the raven?' Sophie said in a low voice while thinking. 'Or because I shouldn't be telling you… do the glasses have a moral compass,' she said taking them off and looking at them. They looked the same as they always did.

'I didn't think you'd stoop to this, Sophie,' Lucy said, and stood to leave. 'The least you can do is refund me.'

Sophie's jaw locked with frustration as she bit down on her back teeth. 'It's not a stunt, Lucy. Honestly. I swear on a stack of Bibles.' Her voice hitched, and she blinked back tears at the icy demeanour that Lucy had adopted. 'I can't believe you are so nasty; I've never seen this side of you.'

Lucy said nothing.

'I know this is the end for us,' Sophie rose as well.

Lucy's eyes widened in surprise. 'It doesn't have to be if you tell me.'

'It's done, I've seen that this is the end of us. I'm sorry I couldn't help you but I hope you'll make the best choice for yourself and that you will be happy.' Sophie returned to her desk, putting the glasses in their case and Lucy gathered her handbag and departed without saying another word.

Sophie wiped her eyes and recalled Miss Sharpe's words that rang true:

'*It is a curse and meant to be a curse, even if we benefit from it. Sadly, you are going to lose friends and it is heartbreaking. But you will gain friends too.*'

Before she had time to feel too sorry for herself, Melino Karta swanned into Sophie's office bearing flowers. Her long flowing dress matched the bouquet colour for colour, and the pink in her hair added a final burst of flourish to the picture. She didn't bother with greetings and cut straight to the chase.

'Who was that gorgeous guy that was here this morning?' Mel asked, eyes wide. 'I swear, you get so many dishy men visiting.'

Sophie grinned. 'That's Detective Murdoch Ashcroft. Drop-in next time you see his car and I'll introduce you. He could use some brightness in his life.'

'Now this is not a bribe,' Mel started handing over the flowers, 'but congratulations! We heard you now own all of this,' she said wide-eyed and turning around in a circle.

The thought cheered Sophie up. She had plenty in her future to keep her busy and occupied. She laughed at Mel's antics. 'Thank you. Word travels fast.'

'We were all questioning Miss Sharpe the moment that man in the Jaguar car left. We thought he might be trying to buy the house… he looked important,' she said as Sophie inhaled the flowers.

'They are gorgeous and so thoughtful, thank you,' Sophie said and went to the sink to grab a vase and put them in water.

'So even though I gave you beautiful flowers, are you still going to turf us all out on the footpath?' she asked, with a grin.

'Merciless me!' Sophie said. 'Of course not.' She brought the flowers back over and put the vase on a small pedestal in front of the bay window. 'They are perfect, thank you. Take a seat.'

The two sat in the front window. Sophie continued. 'I'm going to move in here, eventually. The place is enormous, dusty and needs some serious renovations, but the offices and the arrangements will all stay the same. At least I believe they will. I haven't spoken to the accountant yet, but Mr Saggers – the Jaguar car man and solicitor – assures me they are fine to continue as they are.'

Mel exhaled. 'Phew, well, that's a relief. I'm a creature of habit and I like working here. You know you could take in a housemate or two if you needed extra rent. I might know someone who would be interested and you wouldn't want to be here at night by yourself, unless you've got a boyfriend of course.'

Sophie grinned. 'No, but I'd like a boyfriend. So, a housemate... that's actually an excellent idea. It's not like we'd run into each other too often in this place, unless we wanted to. Would that be you that you have in mind?'

'Yes! How did you guess?' Mel asked with an exaggerated wide-eyed look of surprise.

Sophie laughed. 'Any good with a paintbrush, Mel?'

'A genius,' she said, 'and I'm very good at dusting too.'

'Want a tour?'

'Hell yeah,' Mel said. 'Let's go!'

*****

An hour later, Sophie was back at the desk, behind on all her work. She was grateful to Melino... she had visited when Sophie needed a friend and needed cheering up. Mel reminded Sophie that she had a lot to look forward to and plenty to keep her busy.

Sophie placed a quick call to Lukas and organised to talk in person this evening. He would stay back at work and she would drop into the *Optical Illusion* store. Next, she wanted to do some research on Cassie Delaney. She grabbed her notes and phone, and made a quick call.

'Detective Oakley, it's your female crime partner calling,' she joked when Gerard answered the phone. She enjoyed his hearty laugh.

'Not pulling out, are you?' he asked.

'Hell no, I'm in this until the end. We'll solve this if it's the last thing we do.'

'Might well be,' he said, 'given I'm retiring soon. You got Miss Sharpe's note?'

'Yep. So 11am tomorrow with the brother and beauty queen. To save you a trip want me to meet you there?' she asked.

'And deprive myself of your scintillating company on the way over, no way.'

Sophie laughed. 'Yeah, that would be deprivation.'

'I'll pick you up at 10.30, young lady.'

'I look forward to it, Detective,' Sophie said, and hung up.

'Right,' she said aloud, gathering her wits about her and reflecting on the meetings so far with Cassie's mother and sister. Wearing the glasses, she saw nothing that would help Gerard get a conviction. The father was dead so she would not get to read him, but if he wasn't involved, it would be good to clear his name from suspicion. She was actually looking forward to seeing Gerard again. *Crazy!*

She found a photo of the beauty queens in the newspaper... the finalists and the winners. There was Cassie with her crown on in the middle of the girls, looking up and smiling as if she never believed for a moment she would win. Around her were her friends –Miss Charity, Miss Personality, Miss Beauty Runner-up and Miss Talent – all so gorgeous, so happy.

'Let's see if you've got profiles now,' Sophie said talking to herself which she often did when alone. She sighed when she saw how common their surnames were. It was much easier to find people with unusual names – there was bound to be hundreds of Emily Andersons and Sarah Davis's... not to mention they most likely married and changed their names. She kept the page open with their photo to do a before-and-after comparison and went searching, starting with Kate Moore – Miss Beauty Runner-up and the woman she would meet with tomorrow. At least Sophie was sure of her surname since she'd married Cassie Delaney's brother.

'There you are Mrs Kate Delaney. I'm looking forward to reading you.'

There was no doubt she had the right person. It helped that Kate's maiden name was in brackets next to her surname, but to look at her, Kate was still an attractive woman in her fifties.

She did a quick search for Kate's husband but his profile was just the standard family photo and adventure shots. Sophie struggled to find the rest of the ladies but she wasn't too worried. After all, she could ask Kate about them when they met and what names they went by these days. If they were all still great friends and thick as thieves, then it was likely they were still in contact. Of course, Cassie's demise might have put a wedge between them and created a tragedy none of them cared to remember.

'Let's hope you can tell me something Kate!' Sophie said sitting back and studying the attractive woman. She reflected on her day – a revelation, a friend lost, a friendship gained, and an amazing home to call her own.

'Thank you, Aunt Daphne,' Sophie whispered. She couldn't help but sit and smile. Thinking of Lukas however, sobered her. Tonight, he might give up the role of her protector, it was the last thing she wanted. Sophie turned to study a dove that had landed on her windowsill, looked in at her, and gave her a nod. Sophie smiled.

Was that a message from Lukas that everything would be okay?

Or was it a symbol from Aunty Daphne saying she was with me in spirit?

Maybe it was just a bird, stopping by.

Either way, Sophie was pleased to see it.

Chapter 22

The *Optical Illusion* store looked so beautiful lit at dusk with the light reflecting off the glass and crystals. As Sophie crossed the road to the entrance, she noticed the lights were on upstairs where Alfred lived. He must be in residence but leaving Lukas and Sophie to talk in private downstairs in the business. She tapped lightly on the door and saw Lukas as he appeared from the backroom. He smiled and admitted her. He looked handsome in his grey suit and open-neck shirt.

'Are you okay?' he asked, his eyes scanning her.

'I was going to ask the same of you,' Sophie said entering and placing her bag down on a chair as Lukas relocked the door.

'Yes, I'm fine, thank you,' he said formally. He invited her to come through to the back room. 'So, he knows, Murdoch?'

Sophie nodded. 'He said he has always known.'

Lukas shook his head. 'Bizarre. All those years that Grandpa worked with Daphne, and Daphne worked with

Murdoch, and there was no tension between them and the raven. Now...'

'Perhaps we might be the generation that is in harmony too.'

Lukas grimaced and Sophie laughed.

'Yeah, Murdoch gave me the same look when I said that to him. I have a theory,' Sophie teased and accepted the offer of a cup of coffee.

'Do tell,' Lukas said as Sophie took a seat at the small table in the back room.

'Murdoch, Alfred and Aunt Daphne were all different ages and there was no attraction between them...'

'I'm not attracted to Murdoch,' Lukas assured her with a grin and Sophie laughed.

'No, thank goodness, and you're not attracted to me, but we're all around the same age, all single, all ambitious and territorial.'

'He likes you,' Lukas cut to the chase, 'and he thinks I might be competition.'

'Well, you're with Lucy, so you are not competition and...' she hesitated, 'you may not be my protector for much longer.'

Lukas looked surprised that she knew. He put the cup of coffee in front of her and sat down opposite with his own.

'About that...'

'Yes, about that,' Sophie said, 'You have got little choice, I know, I read Lucy.'

'When?'

'Today. She made a booking under an alias.' Sophie told Lukas about the distressing episode.

'I'm sorry she played that game with you.'

'Me too, it was awful. But the blurring,' Sophie said. 'Do you know what that's about? The first time I read Lucy accidentally, when I didn't know the glasses had power, I saw you two together.'

'Did you?' he cut her off, amazed. 'So, the second time you met me, and before I met Lucy, you knew we'd be partnered?'

'That's the strength of it,' Sophie agreed. 'But now I can't see any men in her future, just blurred shapes.'

Lukas nodded. 'I don't know that you'll find an entry relating to that in the books, but I do recall when Grandpa was overloading me with information, there was something about not being able to read someone if it compromises you.'

Sophie looked confused and Lukas continued.

'Like if they force you to read under duress, you can't do it. I don't know if it is a protection or curse as it could work against you as well,' he said.

'Hmm, makes sense then. Lucy didn't believe me.'

'I'll tell her, for what it's worth.'

Sophie just shook her head. 'Best leave it, she'll think we're conspiring.'

Lukas sighed. 'I don't understand why I have to choose.' He took a sip of coffee and pushed his fair hair out of his eyes.

'I told Lucy the same thing. I tried to relate it to a reverse situation – if she worked with my boyfriend, I wouldn't make him or her choose.'

'Yeah, I gave her the same spiel. For a beautiful woman,

she's very insecure,' Lukas said uncharacteristically speaking out of school. 'It probably doesn't help that I'm not an emotional giant.' He gave a small shrug.

Sophie smiled. 'Me either.'

They shared an affectionate grin, then Sophie cleared her throat and continued.

'As much as I want to continue working with you, there's no pressure from me, so you do what's best for you and Lucy. I'd hate for you to stick by me and lose her and have your heart broken.'

Lukas nodded his thanks, not committing to any decision.

'So, who do you think would be paired with me?' Sophie asked. 'Alfred's well and truly done his years of duty with Daphne. Does Orli want to take on the responsibility? Or would I just be alone?'

'You will never be alone, it's our family's destiny, it can't be changed unless one of the family lines dies out,' he said. 'Then and only then, will it stop.'

Sophie looked at him with alarm. 'So if your line died out but mine and Murdoch's continued, I or my descendants would be in peril?'

He grimaced. 'It's not that simple.'

Sophie rolled her eyes. 'Oh right, but you don't want to tell me that yet?'

'I'm not sure of the details myself,' he confessed. 'But if I step down now, there are several people who could step into the role.'

'Really?' Sophie sat straighter. 'I thought it was just you, Alfred and Orli.'

'No. There are other people whose histories entwine with

ours… Miss Sharpe and Mr Saggers are working with us for a reason – it is complex.'

'This whole thing is bizarre,' Sophie said shaking her head. 'I've been close to Aunt Daphne all my life and spent so much time in her house playing when growing up. Meanwhile, all of you have this secret society going on that I'm not privy to until now. I feel like you must have all been laughing at my antics, and thinking me such a princess.'

'No,' Lukas said firmly. 'We never did such a thing. You were living the life you should be living. But we knew what your fate would be, once Daphne died.'

Sophie leaned forward. 'You know my future?'

'Yes. And no, I'm not telling you so don't ask.'

She sat back and grimaced. 'Spoilsport.'

Lukas laughed.

'I understand,' she assured him. 'I don't really want to know anyway… knowing what is to happen is overrated.'

'Couldn't agree more,' he said, thinking of his own father's death and the burden it placed on his grandfather.

Sophie put her coffee down and became serious again. 'Lukas, from day one of taking on this strange role, I've never understood why your family was divided into protectors and enemies. Why would you even bother looking after my family line who brought about your ancestor's death? This is much, much bigger than just your family line being good guys, isn't it?'

Lukas nodded. 'Yes, and I know you want to know everything immediately. After last time, with the glass breaking,' he said, looking a little sheepish, 'I've vowed to tell you what I can when you ask. But you have to remember that my knowledge is a little wider than yours but not as all-encompassing as it should be. I haven't been a great student or done the preparation to take on this role as I should have.'

He closed his eyes and placed his fingers on his temple.

'What's wrong? Are you alright?' Sophie asked concerned and grabbed his free hand.

Lukas opened his pale blue eyes and nodded. 'I was just telling Grandpa I was going to tell you all I know.'

Sophie frowned. 'In your head?'

'He can hear me if I let him, or if I push for him to hear me.'

'Wow, that's a handy trick.'

'Sometimes,' Lukas agreed. 'Grandpa can help fill in the blanks of the family history.'

Sophie nodded. 'So, what is this, Lukas? What is this weird family history we all share?'

Lukas swallowed and then answered: 'It's a war and it's far from over yet.'

Sophie's breath hitched. 'Seriously?'

Lukas gave her a small smile. 'I am glad you are sitting down because what I'm going to tell you might freak you out.'

Sophie looked keen for the news; Lukas continued.

'You, Sophie, hail from one of the most powerful witches of her time. Everyone feared her, even her husband eventually, once he saw her as she really was for the first time. You're a descendant of the daughter she couldn't save except in spirit, but not in human form.'

Sophie stared at Lukas, frozen.

'We've been expecting you.'

Chapter 23

The history of the glasses, entry three
The reign of Virtue Rayne—March 7, 1606

(Note to book beholder: translated from the traditional word to modern speak by Alfred Lens, 4 September 1972)

I am a seeker of truth and I sought to find out why Saghani's family chose to support mine after she was put to death because of my Uncle Samuel declaring her a witch. Why would her family offer to protect us? That is, one half of the family. Saghani and Bran's twins – Hadley and Harley – were very sure of their opinions. Harley chose to hate my uncle and his descendants including me, which I understand, but the beautiful Hadley vowed to protect us. Why?

From my endeavours, I have found out the truth and it is not as black and white as I thought. I was surprised and delighted to know that Bran, the husband of the deceased Saghani, and my Uncle Samuel, were as close as brothers when their lives were simpler. They grew up together in neighbouring farms, sharing all the joys of boyhood, their studies in their teenage years, and their transition into manhood. They grew apart as Bran travelled with work and met Saghani. My Uncle Samuel, also married, however, he had not an easy life of it, which made him an angry, and sometimes a bitter, man.

Bran always knew his wife, Saghani, had the healing skills, but when he was reunited with my uncle and he first laid eyes on Uncle Samuel's wife, Issbelle, everything changed. Uncle Samuel could not see her for what she really was – she was an ugly old hag who had bewitched Uncle Samuel during his mourning period after losing his wife. Issbelle had won his heart, but she had done so with black magic. Hadley told me that her father, Bran, could not tell Uncle Samuel, his lifelong friend – he was afraid of the consequences to his family, and Uncle Samuel was so happy in that union, who would take that from him? But Bran was terrified for his old friend.

Saghani did not know when she treated Uncle Samuel and saved his life, that he was wishing to die having found out the truth about his wife, Issbelle, and having lost his beloved daughter, Elsopeth, or Sophie as she was nicknamed. She did not know that her healing magic would anger him to the point of vengeance.

Samuel believed that by condemning Saghani and her actions, he was saving my father, Bran, and that Bran too had been bewitched. He told Bran if only a friend had been as courageous to do the same for him, he would not have been mocked and feared unknowingly by the village, and lay every night beside a woman who was fearful of countenance and full of duplicity. He would not have had a child that was half-witch, half-human, a child he loved with all his soul and now had lost.

Hadley shared that her father, Bran, was of course angry and distressed. He lost his beloved wife, Saghani, as a result of Samuel's actions and his twins Hadley and Harley had lost their mother. But in time he softened and understood Samuel truly believed he did the right thing. He thought Bran too had been charmed.

Bran – a bookkeeper – remarried a dressmaker and had four more children to his second wife and eight grandchildren. In time, he had come to dislike magic and to not trust it. It was his compassion and Hadley's sympathy for Samuel given the trickery played on him, that made her decide to protect my family line, whereas Harley added to his mother Saghani's curse by making the raven our enemy.

I have become firm friends with Hadley, she is my protector. Now I wish to seek out where it all began – Issbelle and Sophie, that is, my Uncle Samuel's wife and their deceased daughter, Sophie. Hadley does not think it is wise, but it is part of my destiny. I feel I am to meet the spirit girl.

*****

Sophie stood and paced, her eyes wide, her face pale after reading the first entry related to her ancestor and the girl whose namesake she bore. Lukas watched her with concern.

They heard movement, and behind Lukas, Alfred

appeared in the doorway. He knocked before entering the room. He was always so impeccably groomed and even in his own home at evening – he remained in dress suit pants with a white business shirt but he had abandoned the tie and jacket.

'Grandpa, please come in,' Lukas said.

'I could feel the tension, is everything alright?' he asked, looking from Sophie to Lukas.

'No,' Sophie shook her head. 'No, I've just found out… well… this is why you wanted me to take it slowly,' she said looking to Lukas, and she dropped back into a chair. 'I've pushed it, this is my own making. Now, I don't know what to do next.'

'Nothing, there is no need to do anything, Sophie,' Lukas said and looked to his grandfather to support him. 'We'll just take one step at a time.'

Alfred held up his hands in a calming motion. 'Sophie, my grandson is right. This is an ancestral tie that goes back over five centuries… yes, more than five hundred years. Nothing has to be done today, in one day. Nor tomorrow, nor next week.'

Lukas nodded. 'Exactly. We all have lives; this is just knowledge and circumstances that we adapt to as we go about those normal lives.'

Sophie exhaled and smiled. She gave a nod that was not convincing. 'You are right of course. Nothing is different from yesterday, except I've found out that I am descended from the most powerful witch ever known, and my ancestral father disowned all witches and started a war.'

'Except for that,' Alfred said seriously and then all three smiled and laughed. 'Shall we all sit?'

The three sat around the table.

'How long did it take for Daphne to learn about all this stuff?' Sophie said, pulling her hairband out and running her hands through her hair. The movement relaxed her, and she felt at home at *Optical Illusion* with the two Lens men.

'Years and years, but the difference was, that Daphne accepted her role,' Alfred said. 'So she was in training, for want of a better term, with her predecessor – your great Aunt – long before the day arrived.'

'I, on the other hand, never believed Aunt Daphne when she said I was going to be a clairvoyant and missed the opportunity to learn and to grow with her,' Sophie said.

'Perhaps that is not a bad thing, Sophie,' Alfred, the calming influence in the room, said. 'You have come into the role fresh, with a clear perspective and you have hit the ground running.'

'Well and truly,' Lukas agreed, 'and doing a fine job of it.'

She gave them both a grateful smile. 'You are both very kind. You could have told me it is my fault for ignoring all your support, recommendations and suggestions, and serves me right, so thank you.'

Lukas looked at his grandfather and back to Sophie. 'Well, the same could be said of me, I'm afraid. We're a fine pair.'

'That you are,' Alfred smiled. 'So one day at a time, Sophie, and everything in context. Now, Lukas my boy, how do you propose to go forward?'

'Methodically but quickly,' he added for Sophie's sake.

'Sophie has read Virtue's entry of how it all began, and Samuel Rayne's only entry.'

'Yes,' she agreed, 'I've read that. Samuel's descendant was Thomas Rayne, his son, who was killed for witchcraft, was he not? I must say I didn't read the entry realising the significance of it at the time.'

'Yes, quite ironic,' Alfred said with a sigh. 'Samuel kills a witch and is generationally cursed for it and his son, poor Thomas Rayne, is killed for witchcraft and protecting witches. What a terrible time that was.'

'Not a good time to be a witch,' Lukas agreed.

Alfred continued. 'As you might have read, Samuel's son, Thomas, was from Samuel's first marriage. Then Samuel was widowed, his wife died in childbirth having his second child and he was heartbroken. In stepped Issbelle, the witch. She was Samuel's second wife, and they had a daughter, Elsopeth or she went by the nickname, Sophie.'

Lukas nodded and continued telling Sophie: 'After Thomas Rayne died – who until then had been your only direct living ancestor from Samuel – the book and the cursed glasses went to his cousin, Virtue Rayne.'

'I love that name,' Sophie said and smiled.

'It was quite a common name in the 17th century,' Alfred said, 'and a beautiful name at that. Virtue Rayne was brave and sought an audience with her – Uncle Samuel's witch wife, Issbelle, even though everyone warned her against it.'

'We are yet to read that entry,' Sophie said intrigued. 'Did she meet Issbelle's daughter, Sophie?'

Alfred nodded. 'She went in search of the most powerful

witch of all time and the spirit daughter, and was given an audience with them both.'

'That is what we need to read next,' Lukas said. He produced a folder with a dozen or so pages in it. 'I have made you copies so you can read at home at leisure or call on me if you need me.'

Alfred nodded. 'Knowledge is power. Then you two need to discuss going forward and whether you make that journey together, or if Lukas must surrender his role as protector.'

Chapter 24

Sophie thought about turning in for the night, but it required rising from her couch and going to the bedroom. She was particularly comfortable after earlier heating a TV dinner and enjoying a crisp Sauvignon Blanc glass of wine with it, and streaming a few television programs. Taking in her homely and small apartment, she glanced at Bette Davis asleep on the corner of the couch.

'Do you think we will miss this place, Bette?' she asked. In response, Bette stretched and then tightened again into a ball. Sophie had bought it after her mother died, a small inheritance paid for the deposit and the loan was equivalent to what she would pay in rent. She would have to decide whether to sell it or rent it out now.

'It is definitely time for a change, Bette. I believe we have outgrown our humble home as we've both got older and wiser. You will have a lot more room in our new house and grounds, Bette, but you need to be careful. No going near the car park… in fact, we might investigate some cat enclosures for you that take in all the best spots for a puss cat.' Bette did not reply, but Sophie suspected she was taking it into consideration.

Motivating herself, Sophie pushed herself up from the couch, bid Bette Davis good night and prepared for bed. No sooner had she pulled up the light cotton blanket and turned off the bedside light, she fell asleep, despite the tension of her day with Murdoch, Lukas, Lucy, and her new home responsibility which was so exciting, especially having Mel to share it with as a new flatmate.

Her thoughts returned to Murdoch and his whispered words: "We have travelled together before" and then Sophie envisaged Aunt Daphne's grand home, now hers, thinking of how impressive it would have been on the large estate in the Victorian era. As she drifted into sleep, Sophie saw herself standing in the mansion's entranceway looking over the gardens. There was no carpark because it did not exist then. The streets outside the gate were cobblestone, and a carriage went by, eager faces appearing in its windows to see if they could glimpse the rich and beautiful lady of the house, Miss Sophie Carell.

'Can I get you something, Madame?' her footman said from behind her.

She turned to see the senior man hovering in the doorway, looking at her anxiously.

'No, but thank you, William. I thought I would take some air before Mr Ashcroft's arrival. You may send him to me in the garden when he arrives, please.'

'Very well, Madame,' William said, and discreetly moved away with a small bow which he had perfected over the years of serving the young mistress of the house and her aunty before that.

Sophie lifted her skirts only enough to safely take a couple of steps down to the garden where she strolled in the shade of the large Lilly Pilly trees, along the path as it wound around the pond and fountain. She sat on a bench well placed to enjoy the aspect, her skirts spreading out to cover the chair.

Closing her eyes, Sophie was not sure if she fell asleep momentarily, but she opened them, startled at hearing footsteps coming along the path. Approaching was the handsome, wealthy and powerful, Murdoch Ashcroft – looking resplendent in his dark suit, waistcoat and hat.

'Forgive me. I didn't mean to startle you,' he said. He gave her a smile that always made her heartbeat hasten and as he neared, Murdoch removed his hat, reached for her hand and placed a kiss upon it. He stood straight, his dark hair slightly mussed, his dark brown eyes studying her, while his large gloved hands clasped the band of his hat.

'Did you miss me?' he asked, teasing her as he took the invited seat beside her.

'Of course not, don't be ridiculous,' she said and gave a small laugh at his expression.

'Nor did I miss you,' he countered, and she gave him a sharp laugh and an unconvinced look. He removed his gloves and placed them inside his hat on the seat beside him.

'You look particularly beautiful today, my dear,' he said, and lifted her pale blue skirts embroidered with small bluebirds, to fall across his leg in a manner that, should anyone see, would be scandalous. Reading her trepidation, Murdoch answered: 'Do not be concerned. I have instructed William to allow no one to disturb us.'

'So now you are ordering my servants around,' she said, arching an eyebrow at him.

'I would like to order you around too, but I know better,' he teased, and moved a little closer again. 'You need not fear, I will make for a very progressive husband... to some lucky woman.'

'I can only imagine what that poor woman will have to endure.' She smiled and glanced at the large engagement ring on her finger presented by Murdoch only a month prior. He was leaning close enough to kiss her now on the lips.

Ignoring propriety, she touched his cheek, feeling the hard planes of his face and the rough stubble. 'I have never felt a man's face before.'

'I should hope not,' he answered.

'Need you shave every day?'

'If you like me to be smooth for you.'

'I do, I think,' she answered, continuing to touch him and causing Murdoch much discomfort that she did not understand. 'I shall tell you my preference when I have had you rough and smooth.'

Murdoch swallowed, cleared his throat and recovered himself. 'I shall look forward to it.' He watched her for a moment, saying nothing, and then he said in a voice that seemed to whisper directly in her ear: 'You are my soulmate, Sophie, for all time. We have travelled together for a long time and will, forevermore.'

Her breath hitched, and chills ran across her arms.

'Are you cold?' he asked, making to remove his jacket.

'I am not, thank you.' She looked up at the skies as the

day had darkened and nearby the loud cawing of a crow set a foreboding scene.

'Why are there always crows around you, Murdoch?'

'They've come to take my dark soul to the underworld, perhaps,' he said in jest.

'Don't say that,' Sophie said, her hand going to her heart. 'You will not drive me off.'

'I beg your pardon, I meant it in jest.'

'And if they take you, what then of me?' she asked. 'Will you leave me here, alone, to wander these grounds forever without you, until I too will depart this world from the despair of being separated?'

'Do not say that. I won't speak of it again. It was careless of me,' Murdoch assured her and moved to brush his lips over her hand, but dared to touch her cheek instead. 'Do you wish to go inside, perhaps?'

And then, in Sophie's dream, she was inside in a grand bedroom. The frame of a large four-poster bed was around her and lying with her, leaning over and kissing her neck, was tall, dark and irresistible Murdoch Ashcroft.

'Murdoch,' she whispered.

As strong a man as he was, his frame trembled in anticipation of their lovemaking and with a rush of savage power, he lowered her dress as Sophie moaned desperate for his touch.

'Soulmates,' he said again, although the word seemed to come from all around her. His lips travelled down her neck, over her lips which he brushed but momentarily, and then in the dip near her breasts.

Sophie arched with pleasure and anticipation and whispered his name over and over until she cried it out in passion.

*****

Sophie woke with a start and looked around. She was in her bed, in her apartment in the 21st century, and the clock told her it was just after 6.15am. She dropped back down on her pillow.

How will I ever face Murdoch again? She bit her lip, remembering last night's passionate dream and love making with the gentleman of the same name, different era.

Will he be able to read me like a book? Read my expression and what I've been thinking?

She groaned and rose. 'I need to go for a brisk walk for exercise and put Murdoch, Lukas and all men out of my head for a while,' she declared out loud.

As she leant over to make the bed she had risen from, Sophie jumped back in fright. Something black was in the bed. A spider?

She stood back as far as she could and threw the sheet back. In the middle of the bed, on the sheet where she had been laying, was a single black raven's feather.

Chapter 25

'I'm afraid it's a very busy day, Sophie,' Miss Sharpe said, entering the room and straightening the front curtains as Sophie looked at her day's itinerary which Miss Sharpe kept updated in their shared online calendar.

'Excellent,' Sophie proclaimed. 'I like to be busy and I love the variety, thank you, Miss Sharpe.' She noted the meetings including Detective Gerard Oakley collecting her at 10.30am for an 11am meeting with Cassandra Delaney's brother and his wife, and some readings in the afternoon. Plus, a surprise name for her first meeting of the day – the accountant and nephew of Mr Saggers, Nikolas Saggers, was booked in for a 9am meeting.

'So, Nikolas Saggers?' she looked up at Miss Sharpe for some insider information.

'He's a lovely young man,' Miss Sharpe said, looking particularly sharp herself this fine morning in a navy-blue pant suit with a crisp white shirt underneath. Sophie, by comparison, wore a red wrap-around dress and sensible nude heels, her blonde hair out and make-up carefully done, ready for readings in the afternoon.

'How long have you known him, Miss Sharpe?' Sophie asked, as she stood from her desk and moved to fill her water bottle.

'Since he began in the business. My, he must be nearly 30 now, so twelve years or so. He started with his uncle's business studying to be a chartered accountant under the tutelage of Mr Saggers' own accountant. Now Nikolas heads the team.'

'And he's been looking after Aunt Daphne's accounts and estate all that time?'

'Yes, in a limited capacity while studying and now, he manages it completely,' Miss Sharpe said. 'It is comforting to have someone who knows all the ins-and-outs of the trusts and laws that this property is tied up in.' She sighed at the thought.

'Well, I hope it is a quick meeting,' Sophie said, 'No offence to Nikolas, but I don't have a head for figures and I suspect I'll be in a coma in fifteen minutes if it goes much longer.'

Miss Sharpe laughed and went to put on the kettle.

Sophie expected that if Nikolas took after his uncle, the lawyer, Mr Saggers, he would resemble another Dickens' character, albeit a younger one. As she thought about what Mr Saggers Jr would drive given his uncle impressed in his classic Jaguar, a motorbike came into the parking lot and pulled up under one of the shady trees. A tall man stepped off, took off his helmet, and ran a hand through his dark wavy hair. Sophie watched with interest, wondering which lucky community group was getting a visit from the motorbike Adonis this morning.

The visitor shrugged off his leather jacket, opened a case on the back of the bike and grabbed a suit jacket, and some books. He slipped the jacket on, straightened his tie, and locked his leather jacket and helmet into his bike hutch. He turned and headed up the stairs to Sophie's office. Her eyes widened seeing him coming her way. If this was Nikolas Saggers, Chartered Accountant, he was nothing like his uncle.

Rather, Nikolas was in possession of a firm jaw, broad shoulders, a tall solid build and she gambled his eyes would be dark given the colour of his hair. He was dark of features like Murdoch, but broader, stronger, and as he got closer, she could see his face was slightly scarred as if he had done a few rounds in a boxing ring and lived to tell. Was there a Dickens' character like this? He was more like Jane Austen's brooding Mr Darcy in his stance.

She hurried to sit at her desk and pretend she wasn't checking him out through her office window as he came past, up the few wide stone stairs at the front of the building, down the short hallway, and knocked on the office door. Sophie rose to answer as Miss Sharpe appeared.

'Miss Sharpe,' he said in a warm and deep voice, 'it's great to see you.'

'Nikolas, my dear,' she said, and they embraced. 'I'm so pleased to see you and to know you will be looking after Sophie now. Let me introduce you.'

Nikolas turned and Sophie noticed his eyes widened slightly in surprise – she wondered what Mr Saggers had told his nephew about her. She had to look up to greet him as he towered over her. Miss Sharpe made the introductions.

'Good to meet you,' Nikolas said. 'I bet you couldn't wait for this meeting today... a chance to look at business' accounts, it usually excites most.'

Sophia laughed. 'The highlight of my day and it hasn't even started. Please, take a seat,' she said indicating the small table nearby. Miss Sharpe offered to bring in tea and Nikolas asked for a coffee if it was no trouble. Miss Sharpe assured him it was not.

Nikolas placed his books down on the table and lowered his large frame into the offered seat.

'You need not have changed into your suit coat, we don't stand on ceremony here,' Sophie told him, revealing she had seen him arrive.

'Ah, thank you, but Uncle likes his staff to wear business attire at all times. But if word doesn't get back to him, I'll bear it in mind.'

Sophie tapped her nose. 'Between us, it will be. Unless Miss Sharpe tells.'

'What am I telling about?' she asked bearing the tea and coffee tray. Sophie rose to help, but she shooed her back to her seat.

'Me coming in here in my leathers. Uncle will have a cadenza if I don't look the part,' Nikolas said.

'I told Nikolas he need not change,' Sophie said.

'My lips are sealed on that matter and many others,' Miss Sharpe joked.

'I bet they are,' Sophie teased. 'Will you join us?'

'No, but thank you, Sophie. I have plenty to do, and some bookings to lock in and invoice for you. I'm sure you two will sort things out.'

'I'll do my best not to be too boring,' Nikolas said, drily as if he had read Sophie's mind.

'Boring? Never. Aren't accountants excited by numbers and assume everyone else is as well?' Sophie eyed him suspiciously as she poured herself a cup of tea.

'I've learnt the hard way,' he joked accepting the milk jug.

Sophie grinned. 'Bring it on. I'm ready to find out just what Aunt Daphne has done and what I must do to keep up!'

Nikolas smiled at her. 'I think you'll manage,' he assured her, 'everything is under control. For now.'

*****

Melino Karta could not believe it. Right in the middle of organising a promotional event for her charity group's '*Sport for Every Girl*' campaign, she felt the tingle. There was another witch in the house! In Daphne's house where her community group rented space. Mel was sure of it. She wondered if it was the handsome detective back again, Sophie did say to come around for an introduction.

She made her excuses and slipped out of the office. Management encouraged a walk around the property every two hours for personal health and wellbeing, and Mel was happy to take up the suggestion and do a little spying. Taking her water bottle with her so she could look like she was seeking exercise and a break, Mel wandered towards the front of the offices. There was a smattering of cars – most of them she recognised, and a motorbike that she didn't.

'Nice,' she said aloud and admired the Ducati as she continued around the property on the pretence of seeking exercise.

From a distance, she passed Sophie's window and could see two figures sitting at the table. The glare on the window prevented her from seeing who it was, but she could sense it was male and definitely someone with powers. *How exciting!* She loved working in Daphne's house and soon she would be Sophie's housemate. There was bound to be plenty of witching activity to keep her spiritual roots inspired!

If only the meeting was about to finish and she could be conveniently nearby for an introduction, but there was only so long that Mel could loiter in the garden. After ten minutes she reluctantly returned to her office, vowing to bail up Sophie later for all the news.

Chapter 26

Sophie had surprised herself and chartered accountant, Nikolas Saggers, by not only staying awake but genuinely finding the accounts information on her aunt's property – now Sophie's home – interesting.

'So, in a nutshell,' Nikolas wrapped it up in his distractingly deep voice, 'each of the five community groups pays a small rent weekly. Most of them receive that as a grant so it goes straight from the government source to Daphne's accounts. This money easily covers the house expenses such as rates, electricity, water, garden maintenance, and I skim away a small amount each week for house maintenance – a couple of years ago we completely replaced the roof,' he said by way of example. 'While you have the rents coming in, you can spend your own earnings on groceries, travel, clothes, saving for a raining day, whatever you like.'

'That's brilliant,' Sophie said. 'And if the businesses go, I'll need to cover the costs they are covering now.'

'Are you thinking of getting rid of the businesses?' he asked.

'Definitely not,' she assured him, 'but if they decided to go, I need to know what shortfalls I'll have.'

He nodded. 'You needn't worry about that. We have a waiting list of small groups keen to take up the space if any of the current tenants depart.'

Sophie smile and relaxed. 'Well, you seem to have it completely under control, thank you.'

Nikolas gave her a nod of thanks. 'So, as my new client, shall I accept that as permission to carry on?'

'Yes please,' she said. 'How often did Daphne touch base with you?'

'I sent her a monthly report and we met twice a year. Will that work for you?'

'Excellent, thanks,' Sophie said. She turned her head to the side to study him. 'Can we talk of other matters?'

'Sure,' he said, his large hands closing the ledgers in front of him and he gave Sophie his full attention.

'You know the Lens' men, I assume?'

'Of course, and the lovely Orli. How are they?' he asked.

'Well. Very well. Lukas mentioned your uncle – and I'm assuming by association, yourself – have a long connection with my family,' she hesitated, 'a spiritual connection.'

'Ah, yes,' he said and cut to the chase. 'Why us and why the long-term loyalty?'

Sophie nodded. 'Exactly. I haven't read about your family anywhere in our history, or is it purely a long-term business connection?'

Nikolas's lips thinned and he studied her for a moment. 'Lukas is your protector, isn't he?'

Sophie's eyes widened. 'Yes. Right, so you know about all that...'

'Curse stuff?' he asked looking amused.

'Yeah, curse stuff,' she grinned. 'Did you, well, the Saggers clan, fit into any of that?'

He inhaled and sat back. 'We sure do. A long, long time ago, there was a handsome prince...'

Sophie gave him a smirk. 'That'd be your side of the family then?'

He laughed, flashing a beautiful smile that went all the way to his dark brown eyes.

'That obvious?' he asked. 'But seriously, Lukas hasn't told you yet, obviously. My family descends directly from your line.'

'My line? Hold up... so the Lens' family descend from Saghani's line – her daughter, Hadley.'

'Right.'

'And, the raven...'

'Murdoch Ashcroft,' Nikolas filled in.

Sophie's eyes widened in shock. She sat forward. 'You know about that too? Am I the only one who has been living in a cloud?'

'Apparently,' he agreed, and Sophie gave him a wry look before continuing, making him chuckle.

Sophie continued: 'Murdoch descends from Saghani's line too, but her son's line – Harley.'

'That's correct,' Nikolas said.

'So, you descend from Samuel Rayne's line, the same as me and all the other cursed descendants who have recorded their histories in the journal?'

160

'Yes and no, we're not blood-related,' he responded.

Sophie sighed. 'I just knew it would not be black and white. So, what does that mean?'

Nikolas frowned and hesitated.

'I can take it, I assure you,' Sophie said. 'Just tell me. I wish someone would just tell me something!'

'Okay, but there's no need to panic—'

'Why would I panic?' she cut him off.

He glanced over her shoulder slightly and gave a small nod. Sophie whirled around but no one was there. She stood up.

'What's going on?'

'You asked, so I was checking I could tell you.'

'Checking with whom?' Sophie glanced to the door but Miss Sharpe wasn't anywhere to be seen. 'Were you checking with your uncle, but how? Was he here?'

'No, not my uncle.'

Sophie's eyes narrowed with frustration. 'Maybe I should just go straight to the source and get permission from whoever is at the top of the tree, that I can be told everything?'

Nikolas gave her an exasperated look. 'I'm just respecting protocol, and it was Lukas. He's your protector and I don't want to complicate his life.'

'Lukas was here?' She glanced around again. 'So you have to ask a man if it is okay to tell me what I want to know? And if he agrees, you'll tell me? You two are clearly still stuck in the nineteenth century.'

Nikolas looked confused. 'Do you want to know or not?'

'No,' she said with too much pride. She desperately

wanted to know. 'Thanks for dropping in Nikolas, and for keeping the accounts running, I really appreciate it.'

He stood, grabbed the books and glanced, confused, in her direction. Sensing Sophie had dismissed him, he added: 'I'll send through the monthly report on the last day of each month.'

'Excellent, thank you.'

He extended his hand to shake hers, his hand engulfing her small fingers, and she offered one brief shake before pulling her hand away. Nikolas departed with another look back from the door.

Sophie watched him walk to his bike and swap his jackets, before storing his books and putting on his bike helmet.

'Men and their power trips,' she muttered. She turned and found Miss Sharpe behind her.

'Are you okay, dear?' she asked looking over Sophie's shoulder to the car park where Nikolas was now starting his bike.

Sophie sighed. 'All is in order, thank you, Miss Sharpe. You were right, Nikolas has done a great job.'

'But?' Miss Sharpe asked.

'I am so tired of being manipulated, Miss Sharpe. I feel like everyone is managing me or manipulating me. Lucy has wiped me because she didn't get her way; Lukas tells me what he thinks is best and will give up protecting me because of Lucy; Murdoch has always known he's the raven and is in my company without uttering a word about it, even after he knew I had inherited Daphne's curse; and now Nikolas is drip-feeding me what he thinks I need to know and seeks Lukas's permission to tell me more. Men! I want to know who is in charge of all this spiritual knowledge and go straight to the top.'

'I understand completely, Sophie.'

Sophie gave Miss Sharpe a feeble smile as she moved away from the window. 'I'm just tired and frustrated, I'll be okay.'

Miss Sharpe nodded. 'Of course you will. Strictly between you and me?' she asked and looked around.

'Yes?' Sophie said with interest. Miss Sharpe was her greatest ally after all.

'Let's sit a moment,' Miss Sharpe suggested, and they sat back where Sophie had been sitting with Nikolas only moments before.

Miss Sharpe drew a sharp breath and said: 'Your powers are already stronger than all these men, and I suspect that adds to their cautionary behaviour with you.'

'Really?' Sophie asked surprised and then she smiled with delight. 'Well, that's cool.'

Miss Sharpe hid a smile. 'Most cool indeed. Confidentially,' she warned again, 'I'm sure you've sensed their limitations. Poor Lukas is trying to protect you and also himself, but he is out of his depth but he won't always be. Dear Murdoch is too laid back for his own good. He doesn't want the drama, but he'll use his power if he has to, so he is not one to be taken lightly or disregarded.'

Sophie nodded. She still could not think about Murdoch or hear his name without feeling like she was blushing.

Miss Sharpe continued: 'Then there's dear Nikolas...'

'What is it about Nikolas that he thought I'd panic about?' Sophie asked.

'I will tell you, Sophie, because I believe you are ready to know and I'm sure Daphne would agree with me,' Miss Sharpe lowered her voice, 'she was very big on female empowerment, hence the community groups are all largely supporting women's needs.'

'Girl power,' Sophie said and smiled.

'Indeed. About Nikolas, well he descends from Issbelle like you do, but you descend from both Samuel and Issbelle – the human and the witch. Nikolas, well he descends from Issbelle's other pairing before Samuel. Two very powerful witches.'

Sophie frowned. 'So, he's not human? He looks human.' She gave a small chuckle.

'He's human, like Elsopeth was half-human. But she died and was a spirit child. He too has more spirit in him than the human because he was born of two powerful witches and his human genes are less than what we call normal. One day he might tell you all about it. Have you heard of shapeshifters?'

'Sure. I've seen plenty of movies – all the *Twilight* movies, *Harry Potter, X-Men*.' She stopped short. 'Nikolas is a wolf?'

'No. He's whatever he wants to be. But you, my dear, you are the top of the tree.'

Chapter 27

As Detective Gerard Oakley pulled up at the stone stairs of Sophie's new home and office, Sophie ran around to the passenger side of the car and slid into the air-conditioned comfort.

'Hello young lady,' he said in a fatherly voice and made her laugh.

'Good afternoon, Detective Oakley. I've been looking forward to this.' She smiled at his surprised expression. 'Why, you haven't been?'

He grinned and turned the car out of the driveway and onto the road to Cassie Delaney's brother's home and that of his former beauty queen, model wife.

'I most certainly have been looking forward to watching you in action, closing this cold case, and not spending the afternoon with my grumpy partner.'

'Funny,' Sophie teased, 'that's what Murdoch calls you too.'

'I'm sure he does,' Gerard said and scoffed. 'I thought you would have plenty more exciting things going on than wanting to come out with a grumpy old detective to solve an old case that only offers a small reward.'

Sophie shrugged. 'The reward is nice but I don't care about whether it is small or large, or even if there is one.'

'Burnt out already?' he asked glancing at her before returning his attention to the road.

'No, the money is not a motivator to work on a case. Besides, I'm only working with you and Muddy at this stage. I've got boxes full of letters from people asking for help to find someone. They send some of their items to me in the mail, but I can't work like that.'

'That'd be tough,' Gerard conceded.

'Yeah, some clairvoyants can read by touch, I believe.' Sophie didn't want to complain or reveal too much but added: 'Plus, unlike you with a lifetime of experience under your belt,' she said giving him a wry look, 'my work at the moment is such a big learning curve and everyone is so cautious around me, and slow telling me what I need to know. It's super frustrating. I'm pleased to have a break from the office.'

'And to be with someone who needs the skills you have already.'

She nodded. 'That too, thank you!' She grabbed her bag in a panic. 'The glasses!'

Gerard slowed the car down.

'It's okay, I've got them,' she said and sighed with relief, a hand going to her heart. He sped up again, knowing he didn't have to return to her office.

'You know you said *the* glasses, not *my* glasses. What's that about?' he asked.

'Always the detective!' Sophie thought on her feet. 'I need the glasses to see people close up to read them, but they're Daphne's. Mine are being made for me because I've never really needed them before. So, I guess I don't think of them as mine.' She glanced to Gerard who seemed to accept that explanation. He moved on.

'No cake or flowers today?' he asked.

Sophie smiled. 'No. I figured the beauty queen will play hostess. Speaking of which, what do you know or remember about this couple we're visiting?'

'I was just reading up on them again this morning. It's been a long time since I interviewed them. Cassie's brother, Myles, and Cassie's friend who married her brother, Kate, were, as memory serves, a bland pair. They were never under suspicion and never had much to contribute. Kate was very close to Cassie, she was Miss Runner-up Beauty that year, or whatever the title was,' he said flippantly. 'Cassie's brother was madly in love with Kate, allegedly, and they left the party before Cassie did, and that's that.'

'Was she jealous of Cassie, do you think? Did Kate think she should have won the title and not been Miss Beauty Runner-Up?'

'I went down that path, but she genuinely loved Cassie, so did the other girls in that tight-knit little group – there was five of them including Cassie and they were thick as thieves.'

'BFFs,' Sophie said.

'What's that mean?'

'Best friends forever.'

Gerard rolled his eyes and Sophie laughed.

'Anyway,' Gerard continued as they drove along comfortably together, 'If Kate was jealous, it was just the usual level of green eyes you would expect. Add to that they weren't competing for guys, Kate loved Cassie's brother, so it was in her best interest to get on with Cassie.'

Sophie nodded. 'True. And Myles, did he have any reason to bump his sister off?'

'None whatsoever. He actually liked and loved both his sisters from what I could gather. So, as mentioned, bland as far as the crime goes. Myles did pretty well on the dating scene too, courtesy of Cassie bringing her friends around, but once he met Kate, he committed.'

Gerard indicated and turned into a street and almost immediately turned into the driveway of a large, modern home.

'They do alright financially by the looks of it,' Sophie said.

'Same could be said of you now,' Gerard said with a wink to her. 'Congrats on your acquisition. Murdoch told me.'

'Rich and beautiful,' she joked and made him laugh.

'And modest,' he added.

'Peas from the same pod we two,' she teased. 'Righto, let's see what I can read from the *bland* pair then.'

'Keep that term to yourself,' he warned, as they alighted from the car.

'Maybe. I might get a reaction if I share that you thought they were dull,' Sophie joked. 'They might want to prove they are not.'

'In that case, you have my full permission to throw me to the lions.'

They both looked up as the front door opened and Kate

Delaney came out to welcome them. She was still slim and looked sophisticated in tailored white pants and a navy top with casual white sandals. As far as Sophie could tell, the only difference to Kate now and then, were a few lines the years had added to her face.

'Good of you both to see us, thank you,' Gerard said doing his best to be charming. Sophie was mellowing him. Myles appeared behind his wife dressed more casually in jeans and a red polo shirt, with tan boat shoes. The detective introduced Sophie, and they were welcomed into the couple's modern home made of steel and glass. Once seated with a coffee made from Myles machine that specialised in espresso, Gerard told of re-opening the case.

Sophie slipped her glasses on. She hadn't put them on earlier given Gerard felt the two would contribute very little.

That was a big mistake, and Sophie was just about to rectify it.

Chapter 28

As soon as they spoke of Cassie, images swirled around the couple. Myles's images told of growing up with Cassie and Kim. Shared group outings, birthdays, family Christmases, all happy images. Sophie turned her attention to Kate. She wanted to direct the questions and with a nod from Gerard, intervened.

'Can you tell us about the night of Cassie's 21st birthday? When was the last time you saw her that evening?' Sophie asked.

Kate's countenance saddened. 'It was a long time ago, but that night is etched in my brain forever.' She looked at her husband. 'It started as such a fun night. Those were the days when it wasn't uncommon to have a 21st birthday in the family home with all the generations present.'

'True,' Myles agreed. 'It was a good night, and we knew everyone there, we'd all been hanging out together for years.'

Cassie could see Gerard nodding and smiling at them like he had heard it all before. But the image appearing before her showed more.

'But you saw Cassie later that evening, didn't you?' Sophie said. 'After the guests had gone, you ladies… five of you all met at the creek. Cassie was with you.'

She watched Kate's reaction. Kate laughed and looked to her husband, Myles, then back to Sophie.

'No, what an odd thing to say. Not at all,' she said and straightened. 'We all danced during the evening, we were best friends – me, Cassie, Sarah, Emily and Christie – but then Cassie left the party and as the night grew later, we went our own way.'

'You did go your own way at the party, but you met up again later,' Sophie insisted again. 'The five of you were at the creek after the party, after midnight.'

Again, Kate glanced at her husband and shuffled uncomfortably. Gerard had stiffened and was studying the scene before him with his trained eye. Myles had moved slightly away from Kate to watch her reactions.

Kate swallowed. 'Yes. We went to the creek, we often did, but I don't know what happened to her after that.'

'So you're saying that you saw Cassie after the party? That you left with her? All you girls did and went to the creek?' Gerard asked, his voice controlled but Sophie knew he was angry. Years and years of investigation had gone into this case and right from the start it appears that the four best friends had lied.

'I can see you leaning over her, the four of you,' Sophie said.

'That's crazy. When I left, beautiful Cassie was alive and was really happy, she'd had a great night with family and friends,' Kate assured everyone present.

No sooner had Kate said the words, than new images appeared. Kate was in the front seat of Cassie's car. Cassie was driving and the other three ladies were in the back seat, laughing.

Sophie explained what she saw: 'You all went to the creek together. Cassie drove. Did she not drink that night or was this before the drink-driving restrictions?' Sophie asked with a glance at Gerard.

'Probably before,' Gerard confirmed not taking his eyes off Kate.

'She wasn't drunk, Cassie wasn't a big drinker. None of us was,' Kate said. 'We all went for a drive to the creek together. We were going to skinny dip, to see her night out, just for fun.'

'But then, you all decided you'd share the drugs around. Cassie collapsed,' Sophie reeled back in surprise at the images. 'You didn't know what to do, you were all frightened, crying, you huddled and talked. You didn't call an ambulance.'

Kate stood. 'Get out of my house, both of you!'

'You and the other ladies, are all with Cassie in her last moments of life. You're putting her back in her car, she's dead...' Sophie kept talking. 'All of you pushed the car into the water.'

'Stop! Get out of my house!' she screamed.

Myles was standing, he'd moved beside Detective Oakley.

'Tell me it isn't true? Kate! Tell me?' he said in a dangerously low voice.

She turned on him. 'Of course it's not true. She's crazy,' Kate screamed. 'You should never have let them in, I told you nothing good would come from re-opening old wounds.'

'I'm sure you did,' Gerard said.

Sophie pulled the glasses off and turned to Gerard. 'The beauty queens disposed of Cassie's body. I need to meet them all to get the full story.'

'That's ridiculous and not true. You'll never get us to admit to that,' Kate spat the words angrily at Sophie.

Gerard rose. 'I suggest neither of you contacts any of your old friends as I'll be checking your phone records. Both of you,' he said looking from Myles to Kate. 'Mrs Delaney, you will accompany me to the police station for further questioning.'

Kate sat back down and put her head in her hands. She began to cry. Myles stood nearby watching her, not sure what to do.

Sophie sat and Gerard followed her lead.

'You loved her,' Sophie said, in a conciliatory manner. 'You didn't kill her, she wasn't used to drugs, none of you was. But it was her 21st and you all thought it would be fun to try some. It backfired and then all of you covered it up. Why?'

Kate wiped her face. Sophie could see her struggling with the dilemma – whether to confess or continue the pretence, whether enough evidence would be found if she didn't confess. Gerard put her out of her misery.

'We know she died from a seizure brought on by a drug,' he told her. 'The autopsy showed she didn't drown. We just could never work out how she got behind the wheel, who she was with, why she ended up in the bottom of the creek and whether or not that drug was forced upon her.'

'No, definitely not!' Kate said admitting to her

involvement. She exhaled and her shoulders slumped. She turned her attention to Sophie. 'We loved her, we always will.'

'I know. You were frightened,' Sophie said, reading her, and understanding the fear of the young women at the start of their adult lives. She tried to offer a little empathy to encourage Kate to talk more of what happened that night.

'We didn't kill her,' Kate said.

Gerard's jaw was locked in anger, his eyes narrowed. 'You all provided an alibi for each other, and abundant proof of how tight you all were as friends. You misled us, derailed the investigation.'

Kate sobbed and Gerard continued. 'You might not have killed Cassie, but by concealing her death, you caused significant anguish, especially to Cassie and Myles' father who was seen as a guilty party and wore the stigma to the point he took his life.'

Kate choked with emotion and looked at her husband. 'I am so sorry, we never thought about the consequences.'

Myles said nothing, his face masked in shock.

Kate continued: 'I promise, we didn't kill Cassie or leave her to die, we would never have done that. We never meant for your dad...' her words trailed off.

Myles continued to stare at her wide-eyed, still reeling from the revelations.

Kate cleared her throat and continued: 'The five of us snuck away to the river, we'd been there a thousand times before,' she said looking at Gerard and Sophie. 'We had some drugs, cheap stuff we were given. I don't know what was in it, none of us did. People gave us stuff all the time, anything we wanted really because we were popular and we'd won the pageant.' She sniffed. 'We thought it would be fun to do something risqué on our 21st birthday and Cassie was the last to turn 21. She overdosed or reacted to it, I don't know, but we panicked. We thought it might ruin all of our futures and we didn't want Cassie's parents to know what she did. Cassie would hate that; they would never understand why she did it.' She looked at Myles who gave a small nod in agreement.

'So, you tried to make it look like an accident?' Gerard asked.

Kate shook her head. 'We didn't know what we were doing. We thought we could make it look like she had skidded off the road into the creek and drowned, it would be easier for her family to accept and bring no shame to Cassie. I'd want her to do that for me.'

She stopped to steady herself before continuing: 'We put Cassie back behind the wheel, put her car in neutral and pushed the car into the water.' Her voice hitched. 'It was horrendous watching it sink. I've never, ever, gotten over that, never will.' She gave a small wail of pain and then regathered herself. 'It was such a relief when she was found and could be buried.'

'I know,' Sophie said. 'I saw that.'

'We loved her. I promise we did not hurt her.'

Gerard sighed. He looked at Sophie. She gave him a sympathetic smile – it seemed too easy now… the least suspecting of all Cassie's wide network contributed to the mystery of her death.

It was an accidental overdose hidden by four close friends, the beauty queens. Now it was over.

Chapter 29

That night, Sophie sat with Bette Davis on her couch and pulled out the wad of pages Lukas had given her to read, copied from her ancestors' family record. She had been keen to get to them and to learn more about her namesake ancestor, but she was also exhausted, burnt out, and dealing with too much at once. She had been warned, now Sophie understood why everyone wanted her to take it slowly.

'It was a good day, Bette,' she told her white Persian cat. 'We've given several people some peace.'

Bette looked up, licked a paw and returned to her slumber. Just as Sophie was about to begin reading, there was a knock at the door. She wasn't expecting anyone, and she hoped it was Lucy coming to say she was sorry and all was well again between them. Sophie rose and glanced through the peephole in her door and stepped back surprised.

It was him! Murdoch Ashcroft and it was the first time Sophie had seen him since *that* dream. She placed her forehead on the door, took a deep breath and then stepping back, undid the chain and lock and swung the door open, trying to look as natural and relaxed as possible.

'Murdoch!' she said, sizing up the handsome detective in his dark suit.

'Sophie.'

They looked at each other both reading the situation.

'It's a social call,' he said. 'I've come to volunteer my services for your pending renovations, and hear first-hand how it went with Gerard. Can I come in?'

'Oh sure, sorry, please,' she said and stood aside. Murdoch entered her living area and as she did last time, Bette arched up, hissed at him and tore away into the bedroom. He gave Sophie a small shrug.

Sophie grinned. 'Now that I know there's bird in you, I'm surprised she doesn't attack.'

'Ravens are known to be quarrelsome with cats,' he said, with a small smile.

'Quarrelsome?' Sophie smiled. 'What a charming way to put it. I'm having a glass of white wine; will you have one or do you want your red?' she said with a nod to the bottle he was carrying.

'Red, thanks.' He handed it over. 'Sorry to come unannounced.' He eyed her black leggings and T-shirt.

'That's alright. But I'm not dressed for guests. Do you ever take that suit off?'

'Sure,' he said, 'to shower.'

Sophie laughed and entered the kitchen to find a wine glass for him. She felt better now that the ice was broken and if he continued to be his normal laid-back self, all would be fine. She could not but help wonder if he would be as good in bed as he was in her Victorian era dream. When she returned, Murdoch had removed his coat and tie, and undone the first few buttons of his shirt to look relaxed. She poured him a generous serve of red wine and they returned to the couch that Bette deserted.

'Were you missing me given all the time I spent with your partner?' she teased.

'Yes,' he said bluntly, and she smiled with delight. Sophie then saw he was serious.

'Oh, well that's nice.'

He grimaced at her choice of word.

'It gives me a break from Gerard, and him from me. Been accompanying any other detectives?'

'No, there's only so many hours in the day and I've no desire to do more police work. But I have to confess, I didn't expect too, but I really like your partner,' Sophie told him again. 'Despite the fact we were solving a crime, I enjoyed my time with him.'

'Yeah, he said the same about you, the crusty old bastard,' Murdoch joked and took a mouthful of wine. 'It disappointed him that you unfolded the case so quickly, and he and his team couldn't solve it.'

Sophie bit her lip while she thought. 'He was the junior detective on that case, wasn't he?'

Murdoch nodded.

'We both know he would have been doing what he was told. Besides, those women were young and close. They had tight alibis. Who would have suspected them?'

Murdoch agreed. 'Don't get me wrong, he's relieved too. He feels like he's given Cassie justice and he can retire with a clean slate.'

Sophie nodded. 'So what exactly are your renovating handyman skills? Are you good with heights?' she teased.

Murdoch gave her another grimace. 'I don't fly there if that's what you're asking. But as luck would have it, yes, I'm handy. I'm very good at carpentry. In fact, my father hoped I'd be a carpenter rather than a cop, but I had this calling.'

'Did you really? As a young man?' Sophie asked intrigued.

'Yeah, I know it sounds corny, but I did. I've always been a rescuer. I was a surf lifesaver as a teen and I thought I'd be a paramedic, cop or fireman. A cop is where I ended up.'

'Hmm, impressive. I always hoped to be an actor, but I think it was just vanity driven. I love helping you and Gerard,' she admitted. 'It makes me feel fulfilled in a way I never imagined.' She realised they were getting quite serious.

'Then you'll know how I feel,' Murdoch agreed. 'So about us...'

Sophie's breath hitched, then she remembered he couldn't know about the dream. She gave him her best relaxed impression. 'Yes, about us...'

'You know I would never hurt you, don't you?' Murdoch asked, his deep voice full of sincerity.

'I do, now. Because we're friends. But if we fall out for any reason...'

'Then we fall out,' he said. 'Even if your cat doesn't like me, I'm not going to hurt you, ever.'

'What about Lukas, or whoever my protector is, would you hurt them?'

Murdoch hesitated, and then he put his head on the side in a raven-like manner. 'What do you mean "whoever my protector is?" It's Lukas, isn't it? Is he on death row or something?'

'Pretty much. His girlfriend doesn't want him near me.'

Murdoch cursed. 'Bloody females.'

'Yeah,' Sophie agreed, and they exchanged a smile. 'Want to get a takeaway?'

'So you're not going to cook for me?'

Sophie gave a less than feminine snort. 'Don't be ridiculous.'

Murdoch laughed.

'You're not going to take me to dinner?' she countered.

'I can if you like,' he offered.

'Nah,' she said indicating her casual wear. 'I know a good Thai takeaway we can get delivered, plus there's some birdseed in the cupboard if you'd like a starter.'

'Very funny,' he said, giving her a wry look and Sophie laughed. 'I'll get the birdseed while you order,' he joked.

This was nice, Sophie thought, while it lasted. She wondered if Lukas was tuned into their vibe, waiting to step in if needed. Strangely, she felt like she had a chaperone, whether or not she wanted one.

After dinner and before Sophie had time to wonder if Murdoch intended to make a move on her, he thanked her and grabbed his coat.

'Well, come again,' she said casually.

'Thanks, I might just do that,' he said, and headed to the door like they were old friends. Opening the door, he turned to find Sophie right behind him, but he didn't even attempt a kiss on her cheek.

Then the raven did something old fashioned and

charming… he reached for her hand and placed a kiss on it. Releasing her hand, Murdoch gave her a wink and stepped through the door. 'Lock this now, before I leave. See you in the office. Yours preferably.'

She cleared her throat, her mind scrambling with what just happened but managed to say: 'Unless I'm under arrest,' she agreed and saying goodnight, closed the door. She turned the lock and only then heard him walk away.

What was that? The kiss on the hand, the wink… was he in my dream? Was he in my room?

Except for Blain, Murdoch must be the only man who had ever come around and left with nothing but her company. Sophie didn't know whether to be impressed, flattered or insulted. The chivalry was disconcerting, would he now return in her dreams? She went to search for Bette Davis to tell her she could safely come out now.

Later that evening, propped up in bed, Sophie got her second wind and decided to read one of the journal entries that Lukas gave her. She secretly hoped she would have another love making dream, it was most satisfying to say the least.

With a deep breath, she began to read.

Chapter 30

The history of the glasses, entry four
The reign of Virtue Rayne - June 10, 1606

(Note to book beholder: translated from the traditional word to modern speak by Alfred Lens, 8 September 1972)

It took me three months to journey to the place of my uncle, Samuel Rayne's origin. I was not afraid of travelling alone as my protector was always with me in spirit, and many other travellers welcomed me to join their parties as we travelled the roads. I learnt quickly not to say whom I was seeking as the fear in their eyes alienated them from me and then I would discover they were not as welcoming. Thus, after learning that lesson with post-haste, I told those I met further along that I was seeking my family origins and home, and mentioned the Rayne name instead. This was a much more comfortable truth for many.

When I arrived in my uncle's village, I found only one cousin remained in the area – Giles Rayne. He was a blacksmith and was happy to offer me a place to rest in the home he shared with his wife and three children. I assured them I would stay but a brief time. Again, I did not mention Samuel's wife, Issbelle, for fear it would place them at risk. But it pleased me that my cousin raised the discussion. Later in the evening on the first night of my stay, Giles spoke to me alone.

'You know of our uncle's second wife?' he asked hesitantly.

I nodded. 'Yes, and of the daughter.' I did not say her name.

'Are you seeking them?'

'I am seeking knowledge.' I asked if he knew about the curse on our family. He said he knew a little of it, but would be pleased to hear more. I shared all I knew and when I finished my story, he asked: 'So, the curse went to Samuel, then his son, Thomas. Now yourself?'

'Yes, I believe it is passed to one family member each generation.'

'I'm glad it be you and not me,' he said with a small smile of apology. 'But your bloodline is paternal, that might be the difference.'

I thought about it and agreed.

'What do you want to know?' he asked again in a low voice as if the spirits would overhear us.

I hesitated and tried to explain to my cousin my curiosity as best I could.

'There is a journal which the cursed is to keep and as I am now the third to be cursed in such a brief time, I want to write more of its origins. I want to give all sides and perspectives, so that it is understood and perhaps in time, forgiveness and peace might come to the families at war.'

He nodded. 'Do you think *she* will give you an audience?' He didn't say the witch's name.

'I hope. I come only to know more about their relationship and learn of her love for Samuel and her daughter. She must have loved him once, surely.'

'I cannot say,' Giles answered with a shrug. 'But I don't know why she tricked him and blinded his vision of her. I do know from what I have learnt that Samuel loved her with as much love as any man can give to a woman, and he loved the child twice as much again.'

'Have you seen them recently?'

He nodded. 'They walk through the village now and then. They live on the outskirts. Don't ask me to take you there, I am sorry, but I cannot.'

'I understand and would not ask that of you. But if you can tell me where and which route I should take, I would be grateful. I won't return this way so you need not fear for your family, nor my safety should you not see me again.'

He nodded. 'I would welcome in time, correspondence to let me know of your safety.'

'Of course.' I thanked him for his kindness.

Thus, tomorrow, I will visit them. If there are no further entries from me, you will know I have come to my end.

*****

Sophie's breath hitched as she read the last line of Virtue's account. She flipped the page quickly and exhaled in relief when she saw there was another entry and that Virtue had lived to tell. Regardless of how exhausted she felt – the wine had assisted with that – she had to read on:

The history of the glasses, entry five
The reign of Virtue Rayne – June 12, 1606

(Note to book beholder: translated from the traditional word to modern speak by Alfred Lens, 16 September 1972)

I have news to write. What an interesting time I have had, and this is the first opportunity to write my story. I met with Issbelle, my uncle's second wife, the witch. She was beautiful and I thanked her for allowing me to see her in her beautiful form. This seemed to soften her and I believe, given her skills, she read that my visit was genuine and my research sincere.

Initially, it was just the two of us. We met in nature, in a wide park expanse with beautiful views of the forest where she emerged from; I was very nervous. She invited me to sit beside her on a stone wall that served as a comfortable resting place.

'I know Samuel loved you so completely,' I said as a way of introducing the subject and she bowed her head and looked saddened.

'And I loved him.' Issbelle looked up at me. 'Why would I not present myself in my best form for him? I do not understand why I was condemned for doing so? Do not all wives and women present their best selves for their loved ones?'

'I do my best to make myself respectable, I assure you. I don't always succeed,' I said and made her smile.

'As did I,' she said again. 'But yet he was so angry when he learned I had another form. Would you like to see it?'

My breath hitched and she said: 'You are frightened?'

'I am,' I admitted to her, and she nodded.

'You are also very honest and open. I shall stand further away from you and I promise you I will not change again without your permission.'

She stood and walked further away. I know she could have been at my side in seconds, she is after all a very skilled witch, but again, she was respectful and kind. I understood why Samuel loved her and I felt torn between how the village had condemned her for trickery when that might not have been the case.

She watched me and I nodded my consent. She transformed. I reeled back in fright. She was a small, withered and frightening looking old woman, her nails long, her grey hair long, her back hunched, her teeth sharp. And then, she was back again as the beautiful Issbelle, silvery and magical and she re-joined me.

'Thank you,' I said to her. 'I am sorry we humans are so fearful of…' I stumbled for words and she finished my sentence.

'That which is ugly. People attribute evil with anything that is not within our realms of understanding. Giants, freaks, the deformed, we are all cast from society regardless of our hearts and what lays within our souls.'

I am not saying she is without blame for her deception, but what if she wanted love, and what if she sought out

Samuel who needed love and companionship after being widowed, was it so bad that she transformed herself? They were both happy, he knew of her skills, that was never hidden from him. Was it only when his child could not be saved or when he learnt the villagers feared her and thought he was being duped? Was it male pride?

I wondered all those thoughts in Issbelle's company and she read me easily and gave a small nod.

'He was a proud man.'

'Why did you not stay in this beautiful form for the villagers as well?' I asked, confused.

'I endeavoured to, but some people could see the real me.'

'Other witches?'

'Yes, and those with spiritual natures who are in touch with their inner eye. Elsopeth, my daughter, has always seen me as I truly am and does not fear me. Would you like to meet my daughter?'

I smiled. 'Yes, please, I would.'

She laughed at my enthusiasm and then she called on the spirit child and Elsopeth appeared. Like her mother, she was shiny and beautiful but her hair was blonde and wavy, her eyes grey-blue, and I was transfixed by her as I imagine her father, Samuel, was before me. Issbelle introduced us, calling Elsopeth by her name of affection – Sophie. She was cheeky, mischievous, and she teased me.

'So you are cursed too,' she said as if it were an honour we had earned.

'Are you cursed?' I asked surprised.

'No, but Mama is.'

'Hush child,' Issbelle said. 'That is not a story for today.'

'We don't get many visitors. Are you friend, family or foe?' she asked, cocking her head on the side and studying me. She was a magical little thing, endearing and playful. How her death must have broken my Uncle Samuel's heart.

I looked to Issbelle and she gave a small nod, permitting me to tell my truth.

'I am related to your father, his cousin. Meeting you and your beautiful mother means a great deal to me.'

'You are very nice.' Sophie laughed and turned to her mother. 'But Virtue can only see the beautiful you.'

'Virtue has seen both,' Issbelle said, and Sophie looked at me wide-eyed with surprise. 'Mama was once very beautiful but was cursed.'

'Elsopeth! You are a naughty child sometimes. Did I not tell you not to tell that story?' Issbelle scolded.

'But Virtue is family,' she said and leaned into her mother. She was more mature than her child-like appearance conveyed.

'Please? I would like to know your story if it is not too painful to recall,' I said.

Issbelle gave a small sigh and looked at Sophie again as if to scold her and then she began.

'Sophie is right. I was once exquisite and vain. The village mage granted me a great honour – to marry his son. But I did not love him and I refused his proposal. Unbeknown to me, the mage cursed me. I woke to find myself in my other form; I was the ugliest woman in the village and district and no man would ever ask for my hand again.'

Sophie hugged her mother, her spirit form strong enough to be present and feel as if she were flesh.

'That is so heartbreaking,' I said and Issbelle nodded.

'I have enough skills of my own to appear as such and win the heart of a man for love, but you know the rest of the story. I lost my daughter in flesh and blood and I lost my husband when he saw me for myself. But I have my Sophie always with me now.'

We spoke for a while of the curse upon my family which Samuel had occasioned by outing Saghani as a witch to the authorities, and then in time, I took my leave. I will be honest and admit that even as I left, I did not expect to... I thought Issbelle might strike me down, but that did not happen.

I stayed the night in a local inn, and began the journey home the next day, dropping my cousin a note to be delivered advising of the cordial visit I had and of my safety. Why didn't Uncle Samuel learn more about his wife and have empathy? Was it pride or betrayal or is there a side of the story – his – that I do not know, and will never know? I cannot say but I hope my research and writings provide some insight and comfort to future readers.

*****

Sophie finished and lay back in her bed. She thought of Elsopeth with her wavy blonde hair, blue-grey eyes – the very colourings she shared. Virtue had described the child as mischievous, cheeky, endearing – they were all the words her mother and Aunt Daphne had used about herself over the years.

What became of little Elsopeth the spirit, she wondered?

Does she still walk the earth?

Am I her?

With that thought playing through her mind, Sophie allowed sleep to call her away.

Chapter 31

Detective Gerard Oakley held the umbrella above his and Sophie's head as they stood graveside in the Park View Cemetery and Crematorium. The weather had been fine all week, and now, when they were with Cassandra's remaining family for an anniversary memorial gathering at Cassie's grave, the skies opened.

Fitting, Sophie thought, looking to her left as a large crow arrived on a branch nearby and cawed loudly. She gave it a stern look in case it was Murdoch spying on the pair of them, and it closed its beak and watched her. Cassandra's surviving family had been overwhelmed and grateful for Sophie's discovery. It had been bittersweet to know their husband and father had nothing to do with Cassie's death, despite being wrongly accused. For Cassie's sister, Kim, it was vindication that she would never have harmed her sister, but for Myles, it was likely to be the end of his marriage.

'I don't understand why they didn't just face the music,' he had said over and over in a confused state, working himself to anger. 'Who hasn't drunk too much, tried stupid stuff or done reckless things at that age? Why torment us with the unknown? Why let suspicion fall on my dad and sister? All that time Kate's living with me, seeing our anguish and was involved in disposing of Cassie's body.'

'We considered their part in Cassie's death, the four beauty queen friends,' Gerard told Sophie on the way to the memorial. 'I was only a junior and was told what to do most of the time, but I have to confess, I wouldn't have looked closely at them. Their alibis were solid, and they had no reason to kill Cassie and none of them was the type to procure drugs. Myles, well he won't get past that, his marriage is probably shot. I won't get past it.'

'It would be hard to,' she agreed. The court would now decide on a course of action for the beauty queens. They were, after all, guilty of covering a historic crime but not causing Cassie's death.

A droplet of water ran down Sophie's back and she tipped the rear of Gerard's umbrella a notch higher. The pair stood a little distance from the group – close enough to hear the priest and pay their respects, but not too close to intrude as if they were friends of the family.

Sophie looked at Cassandra's mother, sitting graveside in her wheelchair, wrapped in a warm shawl and flanked by her son, Myles, who was holding a large black umbrella over her. Sophie noticed Gerard following her gaze.

'I bet this is why she'll die soon,' Gerard whispered to her.

Sophie looked alarmed.

He continued: 'You said she'd have a stroke in her sleep, about four months from now. It's because you've given her closure.'

Sophie considered this. 'Like permission to leave?'

He nodded. 'Her work is done here; she has justice for her daughter.'

Sophie sighed and moved closer to Gerard as the rain fell harder. It was a miserable day for a remembrance ceremony. As the priest droned on in a voice that was neither engaging nor pleasant to listen to, Sophie extracted the glasses from her handbag and put them on.

Good practice, she told herself. Gerard raised an eyebrow in her direction and she gave a small shrug. She returned her attention to Cassie's mum in the wheelchair, Iris Delaney. Sophie's reading hadn't changed, she would soon depart this world. She turned her gaze to Cassie's sister Kim. Her future was happy, and Sophie thought she deserved it. She had plenty of family events to look forward to and grandchildren coming in years to come. Oddly, she was the happiest member of the Delaney family, despite being the child that was least supported and loved.

Sophie moved on to the different faces around the grave. None of the beauty queens was present, which was probably a good thing. In fact, the gathering was small; thirty years had taken their toll; Cassie's friends had moved away, forgotten her, or passed away themselves. It was predominantly relatives around the grave. She looked at the man standing next to Myles, supporting him in the absence of Myles' former beauty queen wife, Kate. She had seen his face before several times. Sophie cast her memory back. He was in the images Cassie's sister Kim had brought to mind, as a young man at the party. He had also been in Beauty Queen Kate's images at the party too, if memory served her correctly.

She whispered to Gerard: 'Who is the guy next to Myles?'

Gerard glanced at the man in question. He was taller than Myles, with thinning salt and pepper grey hair, and a good physique. He looked like a runner.

'Myles's best friend, Patrick McGregor. They've been friends for decades, met at high school. He was there at the party but saw nothing, usual story.'

Sophie studied Patrick. He was looking at the grave and thinking back on Cassandra's life. The images as he thought them, projected themselves for Sophie to see. Just as good as asking questions she thought.

Her heart swelled as she saw Patrick as a young man in his early twenties, very handsome and comfortable with Myles, his family and friends. She saw him dancing with Cassie – beautiful Cassie with her long hair flowing and her face filled with happiness. They were a handsome couple, she wondered why they were never an item. Sophie saw Patrick's face harden and she scanned through his images, like watching a slide show above his head. Her question was answered. He was mixing drugs, creating small packages. He tied a small white sachet with a ribbon and placed the rest of the plastic-filled bags and pills in a small paper bag, throwing the sachet in last.

Sophie snapped back as she realised Patrick was staring at her, watching him. His eyes were narrowed and his lips thinned. He knew who she was, everyone at the small gathering did from the earlier introduction. She didn't care, this was the drug supplier, she was sure of it, and that little sachet with the bow, had he prepared something especially for Cassie?

Why?

Sophie knew the answer. He loved Cassie and she rejected him. His best friend, Myles, was dating a beauty queen, and Patrick wanted to date one as well. He was in love with Cassie and she didn't want him.

She squeezed Gerard's arm and he looked at her, but before she could say anything, Patrick muttered something to Myles and started walking away.

'He made the drugs, he gave a special drug to Cassie,' Sophie hissed.

'Are you sure?'

'I saw it.'

'Let's go.' Gerard started following Patrick, juggling the umbrella over the two of them and keeping his arm upright as Sophie leant on him. They tried to keep their balance on the slippery grass with Gerard reaching for his phone at the same time.

'I'll take it,' she said, freeing him from the umbrella as he dialled his police district for back up. He gave short and sharp directions and hung up.

The proceedings at Cassie's grave had stopped, all eyes were watching Patrick walking faster now and Gerard and Sophie following.

'Mr McGregor, stop please,' Gerard called out in an authoritative voice. Patrick turned, ignored them, and turning back, ran across the cemetery grounds towards the car parking lot.

'I hate when they run,' Gerard grumbled.

'I could chase him but I'm not wearing my runners,' she said as they continued to hurry along, not letting him out of their sight.

Patrick had reached the path and was having an easier time on the firm ground. He continued toward the gate, just as Gerard and Sophie reached the path.

'He doesn't have a car here,' Sophie panted, 'he must have come with Myles.'

Gerard grinned as a police car came in through the entrance stopping Patrick in his tracks. They must have been on patrol nearby, his lucky day. Gerard indicated for the two uniformed police officers to detain Patrick. They hurried to do so as Patrick raced past them.

'Righto,' he turned to Sophie. 'Let's follow them to the station and tell me everything you saw in great detail!'

*****

Outside the interview room, Sophie sipped a coffee watching through the mirrored glass as Gerard conducted his interview.

'You can't seriously think that the word of a clairvoyant serves as evidence,' Patrick said and laughed. Sophie saw the cocky look he gave his lawyer, who in return gave him a brief nod of confirmation.

'No, but it opens the door,' Gerard said. 'I can call in each of the beauty queens and ask them who supplied the drugs.

They've been tight-lipped up to now, but since the cat's out of the bag, they've got nothing to lose. They might have covered for you in the past when you shared a secret and needed each other, but why would they cover for you now?' Gerard crossed his arms over his chest and sat back.

Sophie read all the signs of doubt on Patrick's countenance. He licked his lower lip, looked away and back again.

'Push him on the special sachet,' Sophie whispered, hoping Gerard would ask about it.

Gerard waited and then he asked what she had been waiting for. 'There was a special package just for Cassie, wasn't there? Tied up with a ribbon for her birthday. That was your gift just for her,' Gerard said calmly, and then he raised his voice, 'and that was the drug that killed her.'

'Wait up,' Patrick raised his hands, 'you're not pinning that on me.'

Gerard opened Cassie's file in front of him. He ruffled through some pages and pulled out a sheet. 'The toxicology report from the autopsy.' He waved it at Patrick. 'Know what a speedball is?'

Sophie's interest piqued; she'd never heard the term.

Gerard didn't wait for a response. 'It's a mix of cocaine and heroin, and for a young lady who had never taken a drug in her life, it was fatal. Truth be known, it's fatal for thousands of people who are seasoned drug takers. But you knew it would have that effect.'

'They were just a party supply,' he said, and Sophie's eyes widened. That's an admission! He'd admitted to giving the girls the drug. Sophie saw the lawyer roll his eyes.

'You prepared the party mix, and it didn't affect the

rest of the girls, just Cassie who got a special gift. She got harder drugs than her friends. Why did you hate her?' Gerard asked.

Patrick flinched at the words. The lawyer leaned over and spoke with Patrick who shook his head. Sophie was enjoying watching the drama unfold. She had never done that with Murdoch, he always closed the deal without her.

'I didn't hate her,' Patrick said, resigned. 'I loved her.'

'Ah, young love. The only thing worse is unrequited love,' Gerard said. 'So sad.'

'It wasn't like that,' Patrick hissed angrily. 'I loved her, I always had from the first day I met her. When we were at school. Myles's little sister.' He shook his head. 'I could have had any girl I wanted, you know. I was fit, good-looking, chicks would throw themselves at me.'

'But not the girl you wanted. This girl,' he said and tapped Cassandra Delaney's file. 'So if you can't have her, no one can.'

'Everyone thought she was so sweet and nice, she was a tease,' he spat out angrily. 'Beautiful Cassie. She knew I loved her and she just blew me off.'

'So, because you loved her, she had to love you back?' Gerard asked. 'And when she didn't?'

'She got what she deserved,' Patrick said, his voice low and guttural.

Gerard looked to the glass and even though Sophie couldn't make eye contact with him, she smiled at him. Job done.

As Sophie waited for Gerard to drive her home, an overwhelming sadness enveloped her – the people who loved Cassie most, killed her and hid her body, tormented her family, and caused decades of pain. They covered for each other – how convincing and remorseful Patrick must have been when telling the ladies that he did not know what was in the drugs. The beauty queens believing him, that it was somehow a freak accident from the party mix of drugs. Sophie could only imagine the hushed and panicked conversations amongst them all, while Myles remained unaware of their conspiracy to cover the truth. Especially from his best friend and then, soon-to-be wife. What a web of lies they had set up in self-preservation.

She sighed, love sucks.

Chapter 32

Her protector, Lukas Lens, had formally requested Sophie's presence at the *Optical Illusion* store. She knew what this meant – Lukas was going to tell her if he was staying or resigning his position as her protector. She didn't want him to leave her, they were beginning to work well together, and she sensed he was enjoying it. But she also didn't want him to give up Lucy and then be angry with her down the track – if and when she found love and he was alone.

She could find love with him; Sophie had been sure of that not long after they met. No, it wasn't love at first sight because she was too cranky at being left a set of dopey glasses by Aunt Daphne in her will. She had stormed into *Optical Illusion* as if there was no time to waste and the sooner she got the visit over and done with, the better. By her second visit, she had time to really notice Lukas and to admire him. It was too late. Besides, Sophie wasn't sure that the attraction was just one way – emanating from her. Seeing a vision of Lukas and Lucy marrying in her very first glimpse of Lucy's future put an end to any amorous thoughts she might have dreamed of with Lukas, even if she couldn't see the vision again the second time.

Sophie arrived at 8am as requested, before the store opened to the public at 9am. Alfred opened the door for her, greeting her warmly.

'I feel ridiculously nervous,' she whispered to him, her hand on his arm.

'I understand,' he said softly, patting her hand, his voice comforting. 'There has been a lot of change in your life recently and you don't need any more.'

She nodded and gave him a small smile. Sophie loved Alfred's ability to empathise when needed, he really understood. They went to the backroom where Lukas and Orli were already present, the table set for tea as if that would offer some comfort.

Lukas grinned. 'You wore that dress the very first day you came here to collect the glasses Daphne left you.'

'It's beautiful,' Orli said.

Sophie smiled. 'Thank you and yes, I did, I can't believe you remember that. I thought today might be significant, so I wore it again.'

'I wouldn't have picked you for superstitious, Sophie,' Alfred teased, 'not once upon a time, anyway.'

'So true,' Sophie said as they all sat. 'But these days, black cats, ravens, ladders, glass breakers... I'm wary of them all,' she said narrowing her eyes, and the three Lens family members laughed.

'Haven't we come a long way since then?' Orli said in her light, musical voice and squeezed Sophie's hand. 'Uncle Alfred has handed over his dominion, Lukas has stepped up and shown such conviction, Sophie has taken over and managed it all so brilliantly, and you've inherited the house, I hear. Congratulations.'

'Thank you,' Sophie nodded. 'I am super excited, and as much as it pains me to say, Daphne was right not to give it to me sooner.'

Alfred chuckled. 'Well, she saw the future, so she had a head start.' He sobered. 'Can I say, Sophie dear, no matter what my grandson chooses today, he will always care for you and we will always be here for you.'

Lukas nodded, pleased his grandfather could articulate that for him.

'Thank you, Alfred,' Sophie said, 'I couldn't imagine this journey without you all. It would be terrifying.'

And then they all looked to Lukas who Sophie thought looked so handsome this morning in a dark suit, no tie, a crisp white shirt, and his sandy hair falling over his eyes. He pushed it back as if he heard her thoughts.

'Sophie, I—' he stopped and drew a breath, and looked down at his hands on the table. He swallowed and fidgeted, a nervous act.

She held up her hand. 'Let me save you this distress, Lukas.'

'You've seen what is to come?' he asked surprised. 'Normally you can't see or read your protector. Are your skills different again?'

'No,' she assured him, 'they are not, and I haven't seen your decision. But I think you have made the right one.'

He looked confused. 'I haven't told you it yet.'

'I can tell from your demeanour. You are choosing to be with Lucy. Of course, you have to, I am sure I would do the same.'

He looked at Alfred, Orli and then Sophie and gave a brief nod.

'I hope I have no grounds to regret it,' he said. 'I'm sorry, Sophie.'

'You don't need to apologise, Lukas, not at all. I understand,' she said, curious to know who would step up.

'Grandpa and Orli are disappointed, I've let you all down,' Lukas said.

Sophie could tell his choice saddened them, but there were no recriminations.

'Dear boy, best you follow your heart,' Alfred said and Orli nodded. 'Life is short and you don't want to reach the end of your road with regrets that were within your power to change.'

Lukas gave him a grateful nod but could not speak. His face was torn with emotion. Very few protectors have ever stood down and most had enjoyed their roles with their subjects, being part of something bigger and using their age-old skills for good in a modern world.

Sophie sat upright suddenly.

'What is it?' Lukas asked, alarmed.

'Nothing broke,' she said. 'No glass is flying around or cracking.'

Lukas relaxed and chuckled. 'That's why we met in here. And, I've been practising with Grandpa on controlling my impulses.'

'Ah, what a shame then that I can't put you through your paces,' she teased. 'We were good at pushing each other. So, who is to be my protector?' she looked at the surrounding faces. 'Does Lukas get to nominate someone, or do I, or is it a natural progression?'

'Normally, it is a natural progression and the person knows they are next in line should the time come,' Orli said, 'as it was for you when Daphne relegated her powers to you.'

'Which is why Aunt Daphne kept trying to tell me for years that I was going to follow in her footsteps but I wouldn't have a bar of it,' Sophie said and chuckled.

'She was persistent,' Alfred smiled, knowing only too well the woman he protected for decades. 'And of course, Daphne hoped to make the experience easier for you. So as your current protector, it is for Lukas to advise you of your next protector.' Alfred invited his grandson to speak.

Lukas cleared his throat. 'I believe you've met Daphne's lawyer at the will reading, Mr Saggers?'

Sophie looked aghast. 'Mr Saggers is to be my protector? But he's at least 100!' She glimpsed at Alfred. 'Sorry Alfred.'

He laughed. 'I agree, like me, he is.'

Sophie's face fell with disappointment.

'No, not Mr Saggers,' Lukas said hurriedly assuring her he had not handed her over to another protector that might not see out his term.

Sophie exhaled with relief.

Lukas continued: 'His nephew, Nikolas Saggers. You've met him too, I believe?'

Sophie's jaw dropped in surprise. 'The accountant? The shapeshifter?'

'That's him,' Lukas said, and Sophie could tell Lukas wasn't happy about it.

'You don't think he will be a good fit for me?' she asked.

'I think he will be great, better than me,' Lukas said.

Sophie smiled. 'So you were hoping it would be someone less capable than you? Like when you leave a job and you secretly hope the person who takes the role after you, won't be as good?'

'Something like that,' he admitted and grinned.

'You can't have it both ways, Lukas,' Orli teased her cousin. 'You've taken yourself out of the history books and handed over the reins to pursue love. Congratulations. But now Sophie has a history to write.'

'And we expect to see you here regularly,' Alfred said. 'Not only reading the books and working your way through the chosen one's diaries, but writing up your history.'

'Of course,' Sophie said, 'I always look forward to my visits.'

Sophie saw Lukas's shoulders slump. She could sense that he was not overly sure he did the right thing, and was even a little resentful that he had to make a choice. That didn't bode well for future trust between him and Lucy.

She sat straighter and tried to look brighter and more positive about the situation, for Lukas's sake. 'So, when do I meet with Nikolas then?'

They heard a crash against the front glass.

'Good grief!' Orli exclaimed, and all four rose and raced out to the shop. Through the glass door, they saw Nikolas Saggers pick himself up from the doormat and dust himself off. Lukas hurriedly unlocked the door and let him in.

'You could have left the door unlocked,' he said to Lukas as he let him in.

'Sorry, I didn't realise you were coming the unconventional way,' Lukas said.

Nikolas was a tall and well-built man and looked like the proverbial bull in a China shop or in this case, a glass shop. Nikolas shook hands with Lukas, Alfred and kissed Orli on the cheek. Eventually, he turned his attention to Sophie.

'Sophie,' he said. 'Lovely to see you again.'

'And you, Nikolas,' she returned serve, smiling at his ungainly entrance. 'What exactly is the unconventional way?'

He laughed.

'Still having trouble with glass, Nikolas?' Alfred teased him.

'Just your glass. It's not like glass everywhere else,' he said with a wry look to Orli.

Orli smiled and took his arm. 'I'm sorry, Nik, it is charmed.'

'Yeah, it'd be better if it kept your enemies out, not the good guys.' He then turned his attention to Sophie. 'So, we're to be a team.'

'Apparently,' she said.

'Watch out world,' he said, and laughed with his deep laugh. He turned to Lukas. 'Any advice, Lukas, before I take over your charge?'

'Yes, good luck,' he said and gave Sophie a grin.

'I'm not that bad,' she said with a roll of her eyes.

'That's fine, I've always liked a challenge,' Nikolas smiled.

'Sophie's trickier than any balance sheet you've worked on,' Lukas ribbed Nikolas.

'Hello, I'm here,' she said looking from one to the other and earning laughs from the group.

'Come through for a cup of tea,' Alfred said to Nikolas, and ushered the small group out of the showroom filled with glass.

'So what's your strength? What are you best at?' Nikolas asked Sophie as he took a seat beside her at the table.

'Well, it's fair to say I'm better at entering through doors than you,' she smirked.

He put his hand on his heart. 'Aagh, barbs at this hour of the morning. Never mind, I'm sure I'll find out all your strengths and weaknesses in good time, and you will find out mine.'

'I'm only interested in one at the moment,' she said getting everyone's attention.

'What's that?' Nikolas asked cautiously.

'Are you any good with a paintbrush?'

Chapter 33

Melino rested on the fifth step of the ladder and looked over at Sophie, the paintbrush suspended in her hand as she paused for a break.

Sophie, on her knees and shuffling along, looked up from where she was painting the chair rail in the red trim colour Melino had selected.

'You don't like it?' Sophie asked. 'We can change colour, it's your room after all.'

'I love it,' Mel said, 'and thank you for painting a room for me. I love the smell of fresh paint.' She smiled and took in the lovely grand room with its high white ceiling, big bay window and polished timber floor. 'I've never had a room this big in my life!'

'Me either,' Sophie said and grinned. 'This was about the size of my entire apartment before,' she said and made Mel laugh.

Mel descended the ladder. 'Five-minute water break?'

'Great idea,' Sophie said. 'Let me finish to the corner.' She painted on with only a small bit left to do on the chair rail.

'You'd think with all the witches in your life, one of them could wiggle their nose or something and finish the room for us.'

'I know. What's the point otherwise?' Sophie agreed. 'I love that you are in tune with the spiritual world.'

Mel nodded. 'We go way back, witches and me, not that Mum would let me say that word – *Witches!*'

Sophie laughed. 'It does sound very *Hansel and Gretel*. So, as well as potion making, do you sense things?'

'All the time and I'm working at being better at it. I'd love to work in the craft and have a career in herbal potions and remedies,' she said, revealing a little more of her soul.

'Really?' Sophie looked up with surprise. 'Maybe we were meant to meet, maybe that's why you came to work at the *Sports for Every Girl* office which just happened to be in Aunt Daphne's building. We should talk more about your potions.' She touched up the corner of the chair rail with the cheery red paint.

'That would be brilliant. But perhaps you should try them first,' Mel said. 'Speaking of witches, sort of…' Mel walked to the bedroom window and glanced out. 'Here's one now.'

'Which one?' Sophie asked.

'The tall, powerful, gorgeous one.'

'Murdoch? Nikolas? Lukas?' Sophie asked running through the list of tall, handsome men she knew.

'Show off,' Mel teased. 'Tall and dark, if that narrows it down.'

Sophie sighed. 'Not Lukas, but I wish it was him. We were working together, but he's taken on another project.'

'He was your protector,' Mel said.

'You know about that?' Sophie asked surprised, rising from the floor and putting her paintbrush in the tray.

'Daphne was very forthcoming with me. Don't worry, not with everyone else but we spoke a lot,' Mel said.

Sophie wiped her hands on a painting rag and reaching for her water bottle, joined Mel at the window.

'Ah, good, that's Nikolas, the accountant and my new protector!' Sophie said on seeing the tall, dark, handsome shapeshifter shrugging off his leather jacket as he made his way to the front steps. He glanced at the house and then raised his eyes to the second-floor window.

'He has sprung us watching him,' Mel joked. Nikolas gave a smile like he thought the same thing.

Sophie waved and beckoned him up to the second level.

'He's gorgeous,' Mel said, 'and powerful.'

'Yeah, he's alright,' Sophie said with a shrug and then laughed. 'Okay, he's gorgeous.' Sophie's eyes narrowed. 'You can tell he has powers?'

'Strong powers,' Mel said.

'How?'

'It's a bit weird,' Mel said lowering her voice in case Nikolas arrived and heard her. 'But I get twitching in my fingers and nose when I'm around someone with powers. It doesn't keep going, just initially when they arrive. But I had it around you. It's what first drew me to Daphne.'

'So, you think he's got strong powers?' Sophie dug for more information.

'Super strong,' Mel confirmed, and smiled as Nikolas entered behind Sophie.

210

'Wow, this is something this place,' he said. 'Ladies,' he gave them both a small nod.

Sophie did the introductions and he shook Mel's hands, zapping her.

'Sorry we weren't expecting guests,' Sophie said looking down at her paint-spattered clothes. 'To what do we owe the pleasure?'

'If I'd known you were going to be this messy, I wouldn't have come,' he agreed and then laughed at seeing both of the ladies' expressions. 'I thought I'd drop in and see the place for myself since you asked me what I was like with a paintbrush. This is a beautiful room.'

'Soon to be mine,' Mel said in her lovely sing-song voice. 'I'm Sophie's new flatmate.'

'That's great,' Nikolas said, looking from Mel to Sophie. 'Huge place for just the two of you.'

Sophie shrugged. 'Except during the day when there are lots of people here, but you know that being my accountant and all. Why? Are you looking for somewhere to live? There's bound to be a wing spare,' she joked.

'Thank you, but rest assured I have a roof over my head.'

'Sadly, you're not dressed for painting,' Mel teased. 'But can you use your powers to finish the job for us? We want those rolls of red and gold flowered wallpaper under the chair rail and white paint above it and on the ceiling, plus the red chair rail finished on that last side.' Mel said, waving her hand around as if providing instructions to a renovator.

Nikolas's eyes widened in surprise as he looked at Sophie. 'You're halfway there.'

'Yeah, it's a big job with a room this size,' Sophie said.

'Mel senses super powers, so if you have them, let's see the magic.' She grinned as he rolled his eyes.

'It's the truth, you're a very powerful person,' Mel added.

'Am I?' he teased, wandering around the room inspecting their work.

'So, can you help us?' Sophie asked.

Nikolas smiled. 'What fun would that be?'

'Did we say we were having fun,' Sophie said, wiping paint off her hand onto her paint clothes.

'Of course you are,' Nikolas said. 'You're making memories together, creating something, and exercising at the same time.'

'You can't do it then?' Mel asked.

'Nah, not my strength,' he said with a small shrug and a look of apology.

Sophie and Mel grinned and exchanged looks.

'So, what is your superpower?' Mel asked.

Nikolas thought for a moment, and then joining them in the bay window, he lowered himself on the windowsill and answered in all seriousness, 'I'm great with a spreadsheet.'

Sophie groaned, as Mel laughed.

'You're a big help,' Sophie said and then Nikolas nodded his head and the room transformed before them – exactly as Mel had directed and as Sophie imagined.

'Oh my God,' Mel cried out, clapping her hands together. 'You can do it, that's amazing.'

'It's one of my party tricks,' he joked. 'But only this room, and only because I want a coffee and hope to convince you to stop and make me one. Otherwise, you need to experience the joy of renovating.'

'It won't disappear when we come back or appear the old way with other guests?' Sophie asked suspiciously, thinking back on Issbelle's appearance that not all could see.

'I'm insulted,' Nikolas joked. 'As if I'd pull that stunt on you. Nope, consider it done and finished for all to see, until age fades all but the memories of its two residents.'

Sophie stopped grinning long enough to tease his turn of phrase. 'How poetic.'

'That's me,' he agreed.

'Ooh, I love it,' Mel said, clasping her hands together and turning around in a circle.

'You were right, Mel, that wallpaper is perfect, this room looks great.' Sophie turned to Nikolas. 'Well thank you, that's one room done. Mine next… if you did want to help.'

'That'll be interesting,' Nikolas said with a raised eyebrow and suggestive voice. 'What did you have in mind?'

'We'll tell you over coffee,' Mel said as she put the paintbrushes together near the tin.

'Can't wait,' Nikolas said.

They descended the stairs and entered the kitchen on the lower floor.

Nikolas admired it. 'Art deco, nice.'

Sophie agreed. 'It's Aunt Daphne's original kitchen. It's just that art deco is back in vogue again so I don't have to renovate it.' She indicated a seat and ventured to make coffee for the three of them. Mel brought out a cake and sliced it.

'Baked it myself,' she said. 'Full of magic and mystery. Want a slice?'

'Only if I get the magic piece, thanks,' Nikolas said.

'You're very amusing for an accountant,' Sophie said, teasing him.

'That so? Do you think we sit around all day playing with our abacus?'

'Crossed my mind,' she said and brought over the coffees, and joined the pair at the table.

'I'm here on a mission actually,' he said, reaching into the back pocket of his black jeans and pulling out a flyer. 'It's the *Maga Book and Speaker Fair*. I thought you might both be interested.'

'I go every year,' Mel said, 'I'm always looking for old potion books and there are some great speakers in my field. I had a stand there one year when I was a student, and sold a lot of my potions, but I haven't got time to do that at the moment.'

'There must be a spare room here that you can set up as your potion lab,' Sophie said.

'That would be magic,' Mel agreed.

Sophie looked at the flyer. 'Miss Sharpe mentioned it to me and put it in my diary. What's the big deal?'

Nikolas shrugged. 'What Mel said… just thought you might be interested.'

'Do books fly off the shelf and ghosts fly overhead like in *Harry Potter*?' Sophie said with a smile at the thought.

'Something like that,' Mel said. 'It's too late now, but next year, you could join the speed dating clairvoyant group! It's fun.'

'What on earth is that?' Sophie asked. 'Do they match make clairvoyants together?'

Mel laughed. 'No, it's just a quirky name. The attendees

buy a ticket and then they sit in the stands while about twenty clairvoyants sit in the middle of the room at a desk with one chair in front of them. You don't get to pick who does your reading, but your number gets called randomly to take a seat as it becomes vacant, and each reading goes for five minutes. It runs for an hour, three times a day,' Mel said.

Sophie laughed. 'That sounds like fun, I'd be into that.'

'Exhausting for the reader, if they're the real deal,' Nikolas said. 'But it's good marketing for a lot of them, not that you need that.'

'Do you participate in any way?' Sophie asked him.

'Not this year, but I've been on talk panels,' he said with a small shrug, and then explained. 'It's heavily promoted by word of mouth amongst *our* community.'

'Oh, wow. But what if members of the public arrive and want to go in?' Sophie asked.

'Well they can,' Mel said. 'Most that do come are into spiritualism or a bit of magic or they wouldn't want to come. Everyone's pretty open-minded, wouldn't you say, Nikolas?' Mel asked with a shrug.

'Absolutely. It's also a networking thing for the industry and some of the families,' he added. 'I suspect the Lens family will be there during the day. Orli often has a display of crystals and matches people with the best one for them.'

Sophie brightened. 'Sounds intriguing.'

'Let's go together then, all of us,' Mel said and clapped her hands.

'I'm helping a friend set up her display early tomorrow morning, so I'm bound to see you there,' Nikolas said.

Friend, Sophie mused. *Girlfriend?* Mel just asked.

'Girlfriend or soon to be?' she teased, biting her lip.

'Neither, she is just a friend,' he answered straight-faced.

'Mel knows about my protector,' Sophie said. 'So, can I ask, does your wife or current girlfriend object to you looking out for me and taking on the role of my protector?'

'I have neither,' he said, drinking a mouthful of his coffee. 'But I assure you, unlike Lukas, I will not be giving up my responsibilities or be given an ultimatum to do so. If there's no trust there, then it's not going to last a lifetime.'

Sophie nodded. 'Thanks.'

'Speaking of protector, the reason I asked if you were going to the *Maga Book and Speaker Fair* is that I'll need to be on alert if you are.'

'Why?' she frowned.

'The family lines that I mentioned before can sometimes get a bit testy... I'm not sure if the raven will be attending.'

'Doubt it,' Sophie said thinking of Murdoch. She couldn't imagine him there.

'Plus, there are sometimes petty jealousies and word of mouth will have spread that you're now in Daphne's role and your skills are being talked about.'

'Do you think I should stay away?' Sophie asked.

'Hell no, bring it on,' he joked. 'Bring your glasses in case you get the chance to take part, why not?'

'Great,' she said, caught up in his enthusiasm.

'Besides,' he said, 'we've got to work together sometime, so what's the worst that can happen?'

'A spell, a slaying or a curse,' Mel said.

'There you go then,' Nikolas said. He laughed seeing

Sophie's grimace. 'We're teasing you. It's just a book and speaker fair. You'll enjoy it. C'mon, let's check out your bedroom and you can tell me your inspiration,' he said as they finished their coffees.

'Arabian nights,' she said and smiled at his expression. 'Just kidding, I got you this time. Of course I don't want it set up so I look like I'm going to be entertaining every night and killing them the next morning like the king of the great empire.'

'God, I hope not,' Mel said, 'it's a big place but we can only bury so many bodies.'

'You're both freaking me out,' Nikolas said, following them upstairs.

'No, I want it all white with a white doona and pillows, and a white picket fence around my bed, and one large wall featuring sunflowers on a hill,' Sophie said and smiled at the thought. She saw Nikolas's raised eyebrows and knew she had him right where she wanted him – unsuspecting.

Chapter 34

The atmosphere at the *Maga Book and Speaker Fair was* exciting and Mel squealed with delight as they entered brandishing their tickets. Dressed casually in jeans and a red shirt, Sophie looked tame next to Mel in her loud coloured pants and bright pink top.

'Plan of action,' Mel said. 'Let's go to the book section first in case there's something great there we don't want to miss, then we can wander around the displays and hear the talks,' Mel said.

'Great plan, lead on,' Sophie agreed.

After thirty minutes of browsing and several books selected by both ladies, they entered the great hall with wall to wall stands and a large stage at the end where a panel were currently debating if astrology can determine your witch type.

Sophie heard a cry behind her and turned sharply to find a large middle-aged woman with an equally large pile of hair on top of her head smiling at Sophie.

'Oh my,' she said, 'you're the clairvoyant that saved that

child recently… Sophie?' she looked to Mel to confirm she was right and Mel nodded enthusiastically.

'Sophie Carell and this is my friend, Melino Karta,' Sophie said and offered her hand to shake.

'June Weatherbetter,' the lady said shaking both ladies' hands in turn, enthusiastically. 'I'm one of the organisers. Oh my, would you be open to participating today?'

Sophie glanced at Mel noting her encouraging look, and then back to June.

'Why not, what did you have in mind?' Sophie asked.

'Well, I have the perfect thing,' June beamed. 'We did it a few years back with Trent Traymore – you know the internationally successful clairvoyant?'

'Of course,' Sophie said. She had heard of Trent and his showmanship ways from Aunt Daphne who could not stand him.

'Well,' June continued, 'it's a game we call *Am I Right or What?* and basically we select one person at a time, and you tell them one thing about themselves that happened recently, is happening or is about to happen and they confirm it.'

'So, it's proving that clairvoyants really have skills?' Mel asked.

'It's showing what we're capable of and it's fun and exciting for the audience if they get picked. But only if you were comfortable with that, we wouldn't wish to embarrass you,' June said. She lowered her voice and added: 'We only do it with the most skilled clairvoyants.'

'I'm up for it,' Sophie said, 'let's do it.'

June clapped her hands with excitement. 'Wonderful, Sophie, thank you. I have a cancellation at 11am for our main stage entertainment – *Eldora's Dream Interpretation* has pulled out.'

'Did she have a bad night?' Mel asked, and made them all laugh.

'One can only imagine,' June said dramatically. 'Well, I'll go tell the master of ceremonies now and start promoting it. How exciting. I'll see you here in 45 minutes, Sophie.'

She hurried off and Mel squeezed Sophie's arm.

'You're staying with me,' Sophie told her. 'You got me into this.'

Mel laughed. 'I wouldn't miss a moment of it.'

*****

It was standing room only and a sea of hands waving in the air in front of Sophie as she sat on stage in the main auditorium. Mel sat nearby helping June to select the next person to ask to confirm their question and test the clairvoyant. Sophie wondered if Nikolas was out there in the crowd watching and if Lukas had come with his family. Would he bring Lucy to something like this?

Mel picked a young woman who rose to her feet, excited.

'My name is Holly and my question is, will I have children?' she asked and everyone around her hoped she would, given the look of happiness and expectation on her face.

'Well, to Ms Sophie Carell, our guest clairvoyant for *Am I Right or What?* for an answer,' June Weatherbetter said smiling with expectation and enjoying her role on the microphone.

Sophie adjusted her glasses and quickly studied the images around the young woman.

'You will have twins,' Sophie said, and the room erupted in clapping.

June asked Holly, 'Do you know more than you are letting on by any chance?'

'Yes,' Holly said beaming and pulling the man beside her to his feet. She announced: 'We're 10 weeks pregnant with twins.'

Again, the room broke into spontaneous applause and June congratulated them. The applause was over quickly as the hands went straight back into the air to ask a question. Mel picked a young guy on the other side of the room, making June do a hurried sprint through the aisles before holding the microphone to his mouth, about a head above her own.

'My name is Nathan, and I'd like to know if I will go to university or not. My parents want me to,' he explained.

Sophie nodded and studied him and the room was hushed. She could tell from the images on his right what had been to date, and from the images on his left, what was to come.

'I believe you have already graduated, Nathan,' she said and smiled at him. The room waited as June asked: 'Is that true, Nathan?'

'Yes,' he said and grinned, and the crowd applauded Sophie with gusto again.

'Please, one more quick question, this one I don't know the answer to?' he begged, hands in front in a prayer gesture.

'Sure,' Sophie said, and June smiled, pleased.

'I've been applying for jobs for about three months, will I work soon? I desperately want to.'

Sophie studied him again. She saw him in a business suit, signing a work contract dated at the end of the current month. He was also there at a desk, and in a boardroom with other people, and with a girlfriend. She smiled. 'Nathan, your future looks bright. If you want a quick holiday before you start work, best you do it now because you'll have a job by the end of the month.'

He grinned and thanked her; the audience cheered with delight for him. Sophie could tell her words buoyed him, and she knew she was right. She was amazed how many other people in the audience took her words to be gospel.

Sophie answered another five questions and then the thirty-minute session was coming to an end. She had answered everyone correctly or given hope for the future, which was in most cases already in motion with the subjects.

'Last question for today,' June announced. 'Who will be our lucky last, Mel?'

Mel looked around. A man had been staring at her intently for some time, making eye contact, and this time he had his hand up. She selected him and June moved to his side.

'Your name and question please?' June said smiling up at the tall man with bronze features. His skin looked golden tanned, his eyes were hazel and his buzz haircut made him look tough.

'My name is Jax.'

'Ooh, that's different,' June said. 'Go ahead, Jax, what's your question?'

Jax smiled at Sophie. 'Will I live to see tomorrow?' he asked.

There were laughs and then some nervous shuffling and the room stilled. Sophie studied him. She did not need to look for long, she saw what she needed to see. On his past line, images showed Jax had planted a bomb behind the stage she was sitting on. His other images on the future side showed his arrest and imprisonment.

She stood, the room transfixed and silent. From nowhere, Nikolas appeared beside her and Mel yelped in fright, as seated guests gasped with surprise.

'You will,' she said, and then called out: 'Security!' Two guards near the entrance stood alert. They were not expecting any real action, it was a soft job, they were on hand to deter. Now they weren't.

'Hold this man,' she called. 'Please everyone, leave the building calmly.' Sophie went into an acting role, calm, assured, directive.

People scrambled to get out of the room, others stood, watching transfixed, while many filmed it all on their phones. Jax began to run down the centre aisle but was tackled to the ground by a solidly built security guard who wouldn't be much good at speed, but could hold his own in the weight division.

'We're going,' Nikolas said, grabbing Sophie and Mel's arms.

'Not yet,' Sophie pulled her arm away but leaned in closer to him. 'Nikolas get the police, the bomb squad in here, this room, quickly.'

He nodded and vanished again.

June rushed up on the stage beside Sophie. 'What's going on, what do I do?'

'You need to evacuate everyone calmly but quickly.'

'No! But…'

'Now! Please June, it's urgent,' Sophie insisted.

June nodded. 'Ladies and gentlemen, please stay calm and leave the building in an orderly manner. You will be let back in as soon as we get the all-clear.' She started walking towards the crowds, ushering them out.

Lukas appeared at Sophie's side.

'What are you doing here?' she asked, surprised.

'You need to get out, now!' he warned, including Mel in his gaze.

'I know,' she said. 'Mel, go now, get June out too, I'm waiting for the police. I have information for them,' Sophie hurried her off the stage, following Mel down the stairs.

'I'll stay with you,' Mel protested.

'No way, I'll catch up with you outside. Help June get everyone out, Mel, as fast as you can and you too, go!'

Mel nodded and took charge, she was good at staying calm in a crisis, working with young girls had been excellent training.

Sophie saw Nikolas reappear beside her.

'They're a minute away,' he told her, and then he saw Lukas. 'What are you doing here?'

'Getting her out,' Lukas said.

Nikolas's eyes narrowed with anger. 'I've got this, remember?'

Lukas's jaw locked and he faded from their sight.

'We need to get out,' Nikolas said.

Sophie shook her head. 'We've got time.' She ran to the edge of the stage and saw a duffel bag near the stairs. The whine of a police car could be heard and Nikolas ran to the door to beckon them to the right room. Moments later they appeared.

'We've got this now, thank you,' one of the officers said and with that, Nikolas grabbed Sophie and they both vanished from the room.

Chapter 35

The *Optical Illusion* shop was due to open in thirty minutes, but the Lens family were all in attendance. Lukas laid out a vintage fob watch he was commissioned to repair. He had done a few before, in the past, and loved the challenge, loved their beauty. The inscription on the back read '*For all time, my beloved.*' His mind was only half on his preparation, the other half was in turmoil. Angry, frustrated, and confused. Truth be told, he was just keeping it together, and he was in the worst place in the world for that – the glass shop. Plus, his grandfather and Orli could read him like a book, making him feel exposed.

Opposite, he saw his grandfather going through the usual routine before the business opening – preparing the till, checking appointments for Orli's optometry services, removing jewels from the safe and placing them in the cases. In the backroom, in her appointment area, Orli would be turning on her equipment and laptop, cleaning everything with a disinfectant wipe.

'Aren't you at all angry?' Lukas asked out of the blue.

His grandfather looked up at him. 'It doesn't matter if I am or not. It is not for me to interfere, nor you, Lukas.'

Orli joined them, ready to unlock the shop door. Lukas saw them exchange a look; his jaw locked in frustration.

'She's safe, that's the main thing,' Orli added.

'Nikolas should have got Sophie out of there as soon as she detected the bomb,' Lukas snapped.

'I suspect Sophie has her own mind and does not follow orders unless she readily wants to leave,' Alfred said, diplomatically. 'I'm sure Nikolas got her out as soon as he could.'

Orli sighed. 'Lukas, you must release Sophie now. I know you don't want to, I sense your agitation, but you have made your choice. You are no longer responsible for her.'

'And she is in good hands,' Alfred said. 'Nikolas is stronger than you both physically and spiritually. You have an excellent protector following in your footsteps and taking over Sophie's care.'

Lukas gave a curt nod and focussed on the watch. He felt his anger rising, he expected some support or at least agreement from Alfred and Orli, but apparently, he was on his own. He saw Orli reach for the lock on the door and Alfred shook his head. They were expecting him to lose it, to break glass again and put customers in danger.

'Are you regretting your decision to choose Lucy over Sophie?' Orli asked gently.

He thought for a moment before answering, not making eye contact with either of them. 'I'm angry that I have to pick one or the other.'

'Naturally,' Alfred said, 'but it would take a confident

young lady to let you protect another equally beautiful young lady. Lucy's request is not unreasonable.'

'What if we break up? Then I've given up an experience that is by rights, my heritage.'

'Does make it harder to decide,' Alfred agreed.

Lukas studied his grandfather, immaculately dressed and groomed, the epitome of an old-fashioned gentleman.

'Aside from the early days with Daphne, when you learnt prematurely about my parents' deaths, did you ever regret being Daphne's protector, or wish you didn't have the responsibility?' Lukas asked.

Alfred hesitated. 'It's a little late to be asking isn't it, lad?' Alfred said. 'You've made your decision.'

'Maybe, but tell me anyway, tell me the truth.'

Alfred pursed his lips and thought for a moment. 'There were challenging times when Daphne and I did not agree on what was best for her, and Heaven knows, she was stubborn. But we had some marvellous times and challenges too. It was always entertaining. At times, I worried I failed Daphne, but I was also proud to have served in the family tradition. Mind you, I am more of a historian than you, so being part of the book that has captured the story of our families for generations, meant a great deal to me.'

Lukas studied his grandfather for a few more moments, taking in his words.

'You loved Miss Sharpe,' Lukas said abruptly. 'Did she not marry you because of your role with Daphne?'

Alfred looked surprised at the question. He was not one for indiscretions. He cleared his throat and answered: 'You would need to ask Miss Sharpe of course, but my understanding is that it had nothing to do with it. When we were younger, women did not often have careers and Miss Sharpe was very capable and very ambitious. I was the boss's son; she did not wish to take advantage of that.'

'I hate this,' Lukas said.

'What?' Orli asked concerned.

'Making this decision, making the wrong decision.' He rose. 'I'm going out for a bit.'

'Lukas, you won't do anything crazy will you?' Orli asked.

Lukas gave a bitter laugh. 'Like what? No, I'm just going to let off some steam, that's all.'

He felt their eyes on him as he grabbed his keys and departed. He was going straight over to see Sophie. It was not too late.

Chapter 36

The next morning, the headline was the best marketing that Sophie could ask for: '*Clairvoyant saves lives at fair. Bomb on site. Man arrested*'.

'Sophie, dear, I don't know whether you prevent trouble or trouble follows you,' Miss Sharpe said with a scolding look that bordered on concern. She poured tea for Sophie, Melino and herself at the table in front of the office windows on the ground floor.

'You will be in huge demand now,' Mel said, and thanked Miss Sharpe as she accepted a cup of tea. Miss Sharpe only ever served tea in fine China with a cup and saucer. No mugs.

Sophie looked excited. 'I promise you, Miss Sharpe, I was just answering a few questions from the audience, who would have thought that I was going to be tested and everyone there was in grave danger?'

'Apparently, this Jax character,' Miss Sharpe answered and tapped on the newspaper.

Sophie sat at the small round table with the two ladies

where they enjoyed their cup of tea before the day's activities kicked in. Since the incident yesterday afternoon, Sophie had given interviews to two newspapers, four radio stations and three television networks.

'Do you believe what he said?' Mel asked. 'That he had no intention of detonating the bomb, but in a building full of clairvoyants, he wanted to see if anyone would pick up it was there?'

'I can't honestly say because all I saw was him being arrested afterwards,' Sophie said. 'I don't know if it would have gone off if it was undetected, but he was being a smart aleck, by the sounds of it.'

'And you were the only one who picked it up!' Mel said.

'I wouldn't have if he hadn't asked me to read his future.' She looked to Mel, not sure if she knew how the glasses worked and explained: 'I need questions in order for me to read someone.'

Mel nodded and reached for an iced biscuit. 'I knew he was going to ask something; he was watching me intensely all the time, but he didn't put his hand up until the last question.'

'He was grooming you,' Sophie said, 'making sure he was seen. Quite scary.'

'Very scary,' Miss Sharpe agreed. She looked up and then towards the window. 'I'm afraid there is going to be some trouble.'

Sophie paused and glanced the same way, saw nothing and looked around. 'Now? What's happening?'

Moments later Nikolas Saggers turned into the driveway on his motorbike.

'Were we expecting Nikolas?' Sophie asked.

'No. Well yes,' Miss Sharpe said, 'but he doesn't have business with us today if that is what you mean?'

'That's why he's leaving his leathers on,' Sophie said watching him lock up his bike and helmet, and head towards their office.

The three ladies watched the towering figure of Nikolas Saggers walk up the path. He was fit and had a good stride, a confident gait. On seeing them through the window he smiled and raised a hand in greeting, and a few minutes later came through the hallway to their office. He leaned in and knocked on the door.

'Just in time for tea,' Miss Sharpe said.

'I wouldn't say no. How's everyone this morning after the larger-than-life headline?' he said, with a smile, noting the newspaper on the table nearby them.

'Wowed,' Mel said and Sophie agreed.

'I can't believe anyone would do that,' Sophie said.

Nikolas shrugged. 'There are a lot of nutters in the world. Present company excepted.'

'I'm not sure of that,' Sophie said with a wry look at him, and he laughed.

'Thanks.' He pulled up a chair to sit with the ladies, looking like a lion with three meerkats, and accepted a cup of tea and biscuit, offering his thanks. Sophie saw his subtle glance at Mel and then he returned his attention to Sophie and raised an eyebrow in question. She nodded; Mel could be trusted.

Nikolas cleared his throat and continued: 'If now is convenient, I wanted to talk about our, ah, exit yesterday, and make sure you were okay afterwards.'

'It blew me away,' Sophie said, eyes wide and a little excited. 'I've never vanished before. It's the weirdest feeling Miss Sharpe and Mel, like I was dissolving.' She gave a little shudder.

'Yeah, sorry about that,' Nikolas said. 'I didn't really get a chance to warn you or ease you into it.'

Sophie shook her head. 'It was my fault. If we'd left when you said, we could have walked out. But I wanted to be sure the bomb squad knew where Jax had placed the bomb, to save time looking for it.'

'Very considerate and brave of you, my dear,' Miss Sharpe said, looking mortified. 'Nevertheless, you were in great danger.'

'Everyone was, but at least people got out quickly. I suspect we've all seen enough movies and TV shows to know what to do with a bomb alert these days,' Sophie said. 'We made a quick exit too, as soon as the bomb squad sighted it. It wasn't live, yet.' She turned her attention to Nikolas. 'I have so many questions for you.'

'I bet. But you don't have to know all the answer right now do you?' he asked hesitantly, with a glance to his watch and aware of the last time he wasn't forthcoming and she dismissed him. 'I've got to get to work in thirty minutes.'

'No, that's cool,' Sophie said. 'But I want to know who you are in the big picture of things. I know you are related to Issbelle and Elsopeth – Sophie – but I want to know how, and what powers you have.'

He nodded. 'Sure. I want to know your strengths and weaknesses too, especially weaknesses.'

Miss Sharpe nodded, pleased. 'You must be forthcoming, Sophie, so Nikolas can best protect you.'

She grimaced. 'I don't know a lot of my strengths and weaknesses yet because this is all a bit new to me.'

'I'm most interested to see how your skills vary from Daphne,' Miss Sharpe said. 'But for now, I'm just relieved Nikolas was there and got you both out.'

Mel nodded. 'And that the bomb wasn't live and didn't go off.'

'Oh dear.' Miss Sharpe said, but she wasn't referring to the bomb being live. Lukas Lens' drove his car into a parking bay out the front of their office.

Sophie, Mel and Nikolas all turned to see what Miss Sharpe was looking at, and saw Lukas, in his dark suit, alighting from his car.

'What does he want?' Nikolas asked, frustrated and rising. Sophie rose beside Nikolas. She missed Lukas, and knowing they were going to work together. They were just starting to get closer, to create a comfortable niche, and she loved going to the *Optical Illusion* shop. In a way, she felt part of the Lens family, and if she was honest with herself, she felt betrayed by Lukas's actions. Now she would always feel self-conscious visiting, especially if Lucy happened to be visiting there too.

Lukas ran up the front stairs, they heard him quickly coming down the hallway and he appeared in the doorway.

'Morning everyone, am I interrupting anything?'

'Not at all,' Miss Sharpe said.

'I've got to get back to work,' Mel said with a smile to Lukas. 'Catch you later,' she said in Sophie's direction with her eyebrows raised in surprise. The tension in the office was palpable.

'What's up?' Nikolas asked, crossing his arms across his sizeable chest.

'That was crazy what you did yesterday,' Lukas cut to the chase. 'Dangerous for Sophie, and you should have been out of there long before that.'

Nikolas looked like he'd been hit. He frowned, studying Lukas. 'Is that why you are here?'

Sophie put up her hand to stop Lukas. 'I was never in immediate danger, Lukas, honest. I saw the man had planted a bomb, I also saw him being arrested and taken away in that very room so I knew I had a bit of time. Besides, I insisted on staying until I directed the bomb squad.'

'Nikolas should not have allowed it,' Lukas said.

'Are you her protector, or am I?' Nikolas snapped. 'If memory serves me, you hung up your halo, so this has got nothing to do with you.'

'Gentlemen, perhaps we can sit down and talk about this,' Miss Sharpe tried.

'If I'd known you were going to be reckless, I would never have let Sophie partner with you,' Lukas said rudely ignoring Miss Sharpe, which he would not have done had he not been under duress.

Nikolas laughed and looked at Lukas incredulously.

Sophie stood between the two of them and threw her hands up in the air. 'Hello? This is all very chivalrous, but it is the 21st century and I decide what is best for me. Not you two, and yesterday, Nikolas respected that,' she told Lukas.

'That's how it went down, Lukas,' Nikolas said. 'And this will be the first and last time you interfere, it's not your concern anymore.'

'It will always be my concern,' he said, eyes narrowing.

'Oh good. Are you intending on calling after every incident and rating it?' Nikolas asked.

Behind Nikolas the sharp sound of a window cracking made them all flinch.

'Gentlemen, please,' Miss Sharpe said, concerned.

'Don't push it, Lukas, just stand down and leave now,' Nikolas said in a low, threatening voice.

Outside doves appeared. At first just a few, then more and more. Several beat at the window, a crack appearing in another window. A wind howled, rattling the panes. Sophie looked around, not sure who was creating what, where it was coming from, but the howling was getting louder, the skies darker.

Sophie looked to Miss Sharpe. 'Please go, be safe,' Sophie said, and Miss Sharpe shook her head in the negative.

'I shan't leave you, Sophie.'

From out of nowhere, Alfred arrived at the door. It relieved Sophie to see him, and she saw the same expression on Miss Sharpe's countenance.

'Alfred, you're here,' Sophie said and gave him a grateful smile.

'Ladies,' he said, giving them a nod in their direction. 'Hello again, Nik.' He turned to his grandson and raised his voice above the noise. 'Lukas, you're needed at the shop. Step away from this.'

The large glass bay window in front of them shattered into pieces. Sophie screamed with fright. She ducked and Miss Sharpe stepped back from the flying shards.

Nikolas reacted as if Lukas had shot a bullet through the glass – flinching and instinctively moving in front of the ladies, he held his arms up enclosing them with his large stature.

'Get out of here, Lukas,' Nikolas ordered. Another window shattered behind him.

Orli appeared shimmering in the middle of them. She quickly whispered a spell, the glass returned to the window, unbroken, the doves were gone, but the storm continued to threaten.

'Nikolas!' she snapped at him, and then the wind stilled, the sky lightened.

'My apologies, Miss Sharpe, Sophie,' Alfred said on behalf of the two young men in the room.

Miss Sharpe exhaled and placed her hand on her heart. 'Goodness.'

'This ends now,' Nikolas said. 'Am I Sophie's protector or not?'

Alfred nodded. 'Nikolas is right, Lukas. You have given up your responsibilities and must let Sophie and Nikolas determine what is best for them. You have no place here except as a friend.'

'She could have been blown sky-high yesterday,' Lukas spat out, glaring at Nikolas.

Sophie and Nikolas spoke at the same time.

'But I wasn't.'

'I had it under control.'

Nikolas moved a step closer to Lukas with menacing intent. 'You need to step away from this.'

'Unless...' Orli said, and all eyes turned to her as she appeared in sharper detail in front of them. 'Lukas, should you wish to change your mind, you have until the waning crescent of the moon, and then after that, it is too late.'

Lukas looked to his grandfather. 'You never told me that.'

'You never asked. I had no idea you were reconsidering,' Alfred said. 'Are you?'

Nikolas groaned and rolled his eyes. 'Lucky I've got nothing better to do than hang around on standby while Lukas makes up his mind.'

Sophie shook her head. 'Seriously I feel like this whole process is completely out of my hands.' She turned to Miss Sharpe. 'Did Aunt Daphne have all this drama?'

Before an answer was forthcoming, Miss Sharpe snapped to look out the window. She whispered: 'Oh dear, this is just getting worse.'

The group turned to her and then, yet again, followed her gaze to the car park, where another vehicle had just arrived. 'Murdoch is here to discuss a case with you, Sophie dear.'

'The raven,' Nikolas hissed under his breath.

Sophie glanced at Alfred and Orli, they appeared calm. Taking on board their calming influence, she took a deep breath and exhaled, waiting to see what would unfold. This will be interesting, she thought.

'We should leave, Lukas, Orli,' Alfred said to his family members and Sophie saw Miss Sharpe give a quick nod of agreement.

Sophie watched Murdoch coming up the stairs. He

stopped. He sensed them. Murdoch looked toward the window and straight at Sophie. Nikolas moved in front of her.

'He won't hurt me, he never has and Murdoch's had plenty of opportunities to do so,' she assured Nikolas.

'Perhaps I should ask him to come back,' Miss Sharpe said going to the door, but it was too late. Murdoch arrived in the doorway. He took in the group, and finding Sophie, smiled at her.

'Well, what a gathering,' he said, calmly and with a look of amusement. On entering the room, he immediately acknowledged Alfred.

'Mr Lens,' he said and nodded.

'Detective Ashcroft, good day to you. We were just departing,' Alfred said cordially.

'Good to see you, Detective Ashcroft,' Miss Sharpe said trying to keep his business official.

'Always a pleasure to see you, Miss Sharpe,' he said further entering the room, 'and you, Sophie.'

He turned to the remaining party. The room crackled with energy and tension, and Sophie saw Orli humming a small chant for calm, her hands by her side, her palms flat.

Outside several large black ravens appeared on the window frame – dark, menacing and glaring in at them.

'A meeting of the protectors' club?' Murdoch asked. 'Surely not because I was on my way.'

'No, of course not,' Sophie said. 'You've seen the headlines?' She nodded towards the newspaper.

'Yes, and you should have got out of there right away,' Murdoch snapped back.

Lukas raised an eyebrow in Nikolas' direction. Even the enemy – the raven – agreed with him.

'Everyone's an expert on Sophie's safety all of a sudden,' Nikolas said, 'but yet, I was the one there with her on Sunday.'

'Except for when I arrived to get Sophie out of there,' Lukas snarled at Nikolas.

'A fat lot of good both of you would have done if she was blown up,' Murdoch added. 'You call yourself protectors. She's got more to worry about from you two than me.'

The room erupted. Nikolas lunged at Murdoch; a fireball of energy appeared from Lukas in Murdoch's direction forcing Nikolas back; Alfred destroyed it in seconds.

Orli pulled Miss Sharpe to her.

'Oh, for the love of God, stop this,' Sophie shouted, and the room quietened. The three men glared at each other. 'This is ridiculous. I'm not a child or a needy, swooning woman. This is not the nineteenth century.'

Alfred stepped forward; he had the respect of the inhabitants of the room, even Murdoch. He was also the most powerful presence in the room.

'Sophie is right, our apologies, Sophie and Miss Sharpe,' he offered a small formal bow. 'It is best we leave now,' he said with a stern glance to his grandson, 'we are not needed here. Come.'

'Thank you, Alfred,' Sophie said, 'but I have a question, if I may?' She often found herself speaking formally in his presence.

'Please,' he invited her to speak.

'Can I choose my own protector?'

Lukas and Nikolas snapped to look at her and Murdoch smiled.

'Has that ever been done?' Sophie asked, looking from Alfred to Orli, to Miss Sharpe.

'Yes, it has,' Orli confirmed and turned to Alfred. 'Uncle Alfred may remember from the book who did so?'

'Several of your ancestors, Sophie,' Alfred agreed. 'In one case, there was a situation like this – two protectors, one torn about his role and whether to accept it. In the other case, the subject did not connect with his protector and wanted to change.'

'Do you want to choose your own protector, Sophie?' Miss Sharpe asked.

Murdoch lowered himself on the edge of the windowsill, enjoying watching the drama play out; the ravens outside the window remained nearby like his guardians.

Sophie turned to him. 'You needn't look so smug, Murdoch, given everyone is protecting me from you!'

He smiled in acknowledgement. 'Think of me as not here.' He raised his hands for her to continue without interference.

Sophie continued, turning her attention to the rest of her party: 'I think it might be best if I choose my protector given it is the 21st century and if Lukas is reconsidering?' Sophie said, and Lukas gave a nod signifying he wanted to resume his duty. 'After all, why should everyone get a choice except me?'

'Fair enough,' Nikolas agreed, continuing to stand as a formidable presence with his arms folded.

'I made a mistake,' Lukas said, explaining. 'I don't want

to move away from this challenge. I can't.' He locked eyes with Sophie. She saw in her peripheral vision Nikolas rolled his eyes.

'What about Lucy?' Sophie asked.

'She can make the choice, not me,' he said, surprising Sophie.

'Okay. So, if Alfred agrees, and Lukas and Nikolas are happy for me to choose my protector, then I will happily do so,' Sophie said looking at Alfred who nodded his consent, and then to both Nikolas and Lukas who grudgingly agreed.

'Excellent. Then we shall give you some time to think about your decision, Sophie, shall we?' Alfred asked, always respectful of her will. 'It is a big decision, and there is no need to rush it.'

'Shall we meet back here this time next week, perhaps?' Orli asked.

Sophie shook her head. 'Thank you both, you are the voices of reason and calm' she said to them, 'but that won't be necessary.' She turned to the three warring men in her presence – all-powerful and well-meaning – and addressed them.

'I am very grateful Lukas and Nikolas that you would even want to protect me, and that you would risk your lives and your relationships to do so.'

The men softened and acknowledged her words.

'But I know who I wish to be my protector,' Sophie said, and the room stilled. She glanced at Miss Sharpe and wondered if she knew who she intended to select. Miss Sharpe always knew everything in advance, but this time, she looked somewhat perplexed.

'Who is to be your protector then, Sophie dear?' Miss Sharpe asked.

Sophie turned to the men.

'The Raven.'

Murdoch's eyes widened in surprise and he sat upright.

Nikolas and Lukas looked at her, shocked. No one said a word, as if they waited for her to laugh. But she didn't. Instead, she reinforced her wish:

'I want Murdoch, the raven, to be my protector.'

THE END

Special thanks to:

Karri Klawiter, Art by Karri for creating the beautiful covers for this series; proofreader **Penny Clarkson** for taking on another of my books, and beta-reader, **Mary Fuxa** for keeping me on track and the encouragement to keep writing this genre which is new to me!

About the author:

After studying English Literature and Communications at universities in Queensland, Australia, and obtaining a Counselling Diploma, Helen Goltz has worked as a journalist, producer and marketer in print, TV, radio and public relations. Helen is published by Next Chapter, Wild Hearts Creative, and Atlas Productions. She was born in Toowoomba and has made her home in Brisbane.

Connect with Helen at:

Website: www.helengoltz.com

BookBub: https://www.bookbub.com/authors/helen-goltz

Tiktok: https://www.tiktok.com/@authorhelengoltz

Facebook: www.facebook.com/HelenGoltz.Author

Twitter: https://twitter.com/HelenGwriter

Instagram: https://www.instagram.com/helengoltz1/

Sign-up for Helen's newsletter on her website, for book discounts and specials.

You might also enjoy by this author...

The Lady Mortician's Visions
The Missing Brides
The Fake Child
The Dastardly Debutante (coming soon)

Miss Hayward & the Detective Series (historical mystery/romance):
Murder at the Freak Show
The Artist's Missing Muse
Mystery at the Asylum
The Mortician's Clue
Murder in Bridal Lane

The Clairvoyant's Glasses (paranormal/romance):
Volume 1 – A vision unexpected
Volume 2 – Time has a shadow
Volume 3 – Love knows no bounds
Volume 4 – Fate comes to call

The Jesse Clarke series (cosy mystery):
Death by Sugar
Death by Disguise
Death by Reunion

The Mitchell Parker series (crime thriller):
Mastermind
Graveyard of the Atlantic
The Fourth Reich

Writing as Jack Adams (mystery suspense):

Poster Girl
And the Delaney and Murphy childhood friends' series:
Asylum
Stalker
Cult
Hitched (coming soon)

Writing as Ally Adams:

The Saints team (contemporary romance):
Team Lucas
Team Tomas
Team Niklas
Team Alex

Spies in Love (contemporary romance):
My Boyfriend the Spy
I Spy My Guy

Stand-alone titles:
The House on Findlater Lane (mystery/romance paranormal)
The Forgotten House (historical romance)
Three Parts Truth (mystery suspense)
Morphers (middle grade fiction)

Non-fiction with journalist, Chris Adams:
The Grave Tales series (non-fiction books and podcast).